They were the center of attention

"All eyes seem to be on us," he said softly into her ear. "Is there anyone whose toes I'll be treading on?"

Her teeth bit into her bottom lip. "No," Kathy said angrily.

"But what a boring life you lead. Or is being a mother enough emotional outlet for you? Somehow, I think not."

"Shut up," she hissed, flushing.

His laughter was soft and ironic. "Yes, you're right. This is hardly the occasion to talk over old times."

"I don't want to talk over old times," she snapped.

"Oh, I think we should. You left such a lot of unfinished business behind when you ran away that I promised myself I'd see that you finished it if we met again."

ROBYN DONALD lives in northern New Zealand with her husband and children. They love the outdoors and particularly enjoy sailing and stargazing on warm nights. Robyn doesn't remember being taught to read, but rates reading as one of her greatest pleasures, if not a vice. She finds writing intensely rewarding and is continually surprised by the way her characters develop independent lives of their own.

Books by Robyn Donald

HARLEQUIN PRESENTS
1233—LOVE'S REWARD
1263—A BITTER HOMECOMING
1303—NO GUARANTEES
1343—A MATTER OF WILL
1376—THE DARKER SIDE OF PARADISE
1408—A SUMMER STORM

HARLEQUIN ROMANCE
2391—BAY OF STARS
2437—ICEBERG

Don't miss any of our special offers. Write to us at the following address for information on our newest releases.

Harlequin Reader Service
P.O. Box 1397, Buffalo, NY 14240
Canadian address: P.O. Box 603,
Fort Erie, Ont. L2A 5X3

ROBYN DONALD

no place too far

Harlequin Books

TORONTO • NEW YORK • LONDON
AMSTERDAM • PARIS • SYDNEY • HAMBURG
STOCKHOLM • ATHENS • TOKYO • MILAN

Harlequin Presents first edition February 1992
ISBN 0-373-11434-6

Original hardcover edition published in 1990
by Mills & Boon Limited

NO PLACE TOO FAR

CHAPTER ONE

KATHY TOWNSEND was normally shy, but when she danced the inhibitions so carefully instilled by her mother disappeared and she gave herself heart and soul to the rhythm, wild shoulder-length hair flying in a swirl of coppery-brown, great golden eyes slumbrous beneath long dark lashes. She was not beautiful, her face being too thin with a narrow jawline leading to rather fragile temples, but the unexpectedly cleft chin and sleek golden skin combined with her unrestrained, sensuous grace to create an illusion of seductive glamour.

Music throbbed in her veins, brought the blood to her cheeks and her wide soft mouth, invaded her system so that she was a sinuous extension of it. Her partner, no mean dancer himself, found himself encouraged to greater heights of improvisation than he had ever aspired to before. As the song reached a crescendo he caught her hand and twirled her around and around, finally bending her over backwards in a parody of a Latin clinch.

As soon as she could she straightened, applause ringing in her ears as the rest of the party guests showed their appreciation.

'Hey, that was great,' said her partner, Martin Somebody-or-other, surveying her slender form, his eager eyes lingering on the golden shoulder bared by a figure-hugging bodysuit, then moving purposefully to neat hips and long legs covered by the full skirt she had made in exactly the same deep peach shade. 'Let's do it again, shall we?'

But the music's magic was already fading. That last too-intimate embrace had revealed that he was slightly aroused. Kathy knew she shouldn't feel the faint distaste that cooled her mood so abruptly, but she was not a very physical person and she didn't know how to cope with situations like that except by backing off.

Her cousin Chris, with whom she had shared a flat until three weeks before, used to tease her gently about being Victorian, and try to convince her that it was a compliment when men liked to look at her and touch her, but it was not easy for her to overcome her childhood conditioning and she always reacted with discomfort and embarrassment.

So she gave Martin a slight smile and said in her vaguest tone, 'No, thank you, I need a drink. I'm dying of thirst.'

'I'll get you something,' he offered eagerly. 'Wine? Or beer?'

She smiled. 'Just lime juice, thanks,' she said, her deep voice husky and soft, waiting until he was out of sight before she began to slide through the throngs of people jammed into the large room.

She didn't really know why she was there. No, that was wrong, she was there because Libby Anderson had nagged her into coming. But it was hot and crowded, Libby was flirting cheerfully with a large rugby type, and Kathy wanted nothing more than to go back to the flat she now thought of as home. A man she only just recognised grabbed her by the arm and congratulated her on her dancing; as always, Kathy felt embarrassed by her abandon. It didn't help to realise that it was instinctive, her spontaneous reaction to rhythm and melody. She had always danced, and her mother had always looked shocked and disapproving, talking of wildness and lack of control. That implanted conviction that it was somehow sordid to lose herself in movement still lingered in spite of Chris's efforts to eradicate it.

So now, even as her cheeks flushed a deeper apricot, she smiled and nodded and said as little as possible, and when she got the opportunity slithered on between more people until she was within sight of the french windows.

It was not exactly easy to reach the sanctuary of the wide balcony overlooking the harbour. The room seemed full of giants. Not above medium height herself, she felt overwhelmed, almost intimidated by them, but persevered, excusing herself past another three or four until, finally, she was almost there. Faint tendrils of humid air, sign of a typical early summer night in Auckland, floated across her heated skin. Sticky though it was, it felt blessedly cool compared to the fug inside.

There was, however, a final obstacle blocking any further retreat. One more man, another giant. Staring resentfully at lean wide shoulders and narrow hips above strongly muscled legs that seemed to go on forever, she reiterated, 'Excuse me,' endeavouring to slide past without actually touching him.

He turned, looking down from his six feet two, and the words died on her lips. Eyes of a brilliant olive-green, intense in colour yet oddly opaque, travelled across her face in a scrutiny that seemed to search out her soul.

Wicked eyes, she thought in confusion. Laughing, yet not amused, as though the joke was bitter, and was on him, they were set in a frame of black lashes and brows that winged slightly upwards at the outer ends, giving him a reckless, devilish look.

'Sorry,' he said. His voice was deep, of an unusual timbre, with a hint of strong emotion crackling through the conventional words of apology.

The tip of Kathy's tongue stole out to touch suddenly dry lips, and was hastily withdrawn when she saw his gaze fix on to it. Something odd was happening in her stomach, something even odder at the base of her spine. Although normally graceful, she tripped as she took the last step on to the balcony.

He had quick reactions; his hands fastened around her shoulders, pulling her up and too close.

'Are you all right?' He sounded shaken, almost as shaken as she was.

His hands had dropped away almost immediately, but she still felt them burning into her skin. In a voice even huskier than normal she essayed a little laugh, but gave up on it when it threatened to wobble. 'I'm sorry,' she said. 'I don't normally fall over my feet.'

'No, I watched you dancing. Grace and fire and passion personified.'

She hoped fervently that she was far enough out of the room for the friendly darkness to hide the heat scalding her cheeks. Some note, some faint inflexion in the words, made her wonder if he thought she was an exhibitionist.

Almost she apologised, but pride brought her head up and straightened her already very straight back. 'Thank you,' she said, her voice cooling perceptibly.

'You don't believe me? Why not? You must realise how you look when you dance.' He had followed her out on to the wide wooden deck, but he wasn't admiring the stunning view over Rangitoto and Music Point and the lower reaches of the Waitemata harbour. Instead, she could feel those strange piercing eyes on her, probing through the darkness.

Moving a little further away, she took a deep breath before she could answer. 'How could I? I've never seen myself.'

A flash of white indicated a narrow smile. 'No, I suppose not. But the applause should have convinced you that when you dance you're like something from another dimension, brought to life by the music, living only to express it through movement.'

'Thank you,' she said again, uncertain of exactly how to cope with this rather fulsome flattery. 'I enjoy dancing and I know I have a certain small talent, but don't you think you're exaggerating just a little? Compliments like that apply to Nureyev or Fonteyn. I haven't had any training at all, and I dance solely for my own amusement.'

'And surely to give pleasure to others,' he suggested urbanely.

She shrugged, angry with what he was implying, yet still trapped by the flare of attraction that had flamed so suddenly when his eyes met hers. She could feel it now, coiling through her body, slow and sweet and dangerous, the first languid sweep of desire. 'That's a bonus, although it's not one I look for. I dance for selfish reasons, I'm afraid.'

He laughed softly but with a metallic undertone that robbed the sound of any humour. 'I imagine your boyfriend doesn't think so.'

'My boyfriend—oh, you mean Martin? He's not my boyfriend.'

'That was a fairly intimate embrace you indulged in.'

Temper sparked her words. 'One I broke out of as soon as I could without making him look a fool, although I don't suppose you'd accept that. I can't believe that a total stranger is telling me off because of my behaviour! Or that I'm trying to excuse myself! What are you, some kind of religious zealot—a puritan?'

'Far from it,' he said brusquely, catching her arm as she swung to retreat inside. 'But the reason I'm behaving like a fool is the same reason you're making excuses— I didn't like seeing that damned young puppy force himself on you because I wanted to do it myself, and you want it too.'

'Now, wait——' Her words died stillborn as he pulled her into his arms. She could feel the tautness of his lean body against her but this time she wasn't made uneasy by such open hunger. Indeed, it evoked an answering response, a sharp tug at her nerves that made her swallow convulsively.

Her eyes flew up to meet his, which were dark, almost sombre, yet lit by a febrile spark of excitement. She whispered, 'I don't want this. I don't know what it is.'

'Neither do I,' he said, equally low, 'but I know I'd die to kiss you. What's your name?'

'Kathy Townsend. What's yours?'

'André Hunter.'

The name was vaguely familiar, but she was too absorbed in his physical presence and her own astonishing reaction to wonder where she had heard it before. With her sight reconciled to the darkness she realised that she was staring in open hunger, eyes dilated, skin prickling as though a layer had been stripped away so that she was exposed almost painfully to the world.

He was staring back at her. Tonelessly he said, 'You have incredible eyes. I noticed them before, blazing gold as you drove every man mad wondering if they promised what he thought they did. Topazes, made incandescent by orange starbursts. I've never seen such eyes before.'

'Cat's eyes,' she said thickly, struggling to hang on to her composure. Drawing in a deep lungful of the damp air, she shivered in spite of the wave of heat rolling through her. Some distant sensible part of her brain warned her that it would be totally humiliating if he realised how he affected her, so she finished dismissively in a brittle voice that strove for sophistication. 'Most cats have eyes just like mine.'

'Spellbinding, mysterious eyes,' he corrected softly, 'glowing with fire and a wild vitality. Dangerous, sultry, beguiling eyes.'

Swallowing the lump in her throat, she retorted with light scorn, 'A nice line. I'll bet it works well.'

'It is not a line,' he said, smiling. In the shifting patterns of the light from inside it was difficult to see what expression touched the striking aquiline features, but again she was sure there was no humour in it.

His arms were loose across her back but she knew without a doubt that if she made an attempt to pull away they would tighten. Some dim remnant of common sense told her that if anyone stumbled out on them they would look utterly stupid, staring into each other's eyes as though bound together by some mysterious alchemy, so still that she could feel her life force throbbing through her body in a deep rhythm, see an answering pulse in the strong brown column of his neck.

Her voice deepened to a croak. 'I—I think I'm cold.'

And realised immediately that she had played into his hands. With a mocking undertone he said, 'But the whole of New Zealand is suffering from a heatwave. Never mind, I can warm you.'

She watched, eyes widening, as his head came towards her, the arrogant determination of his features the last thing that impinged before her lashes fluttered down. Her breath stopped in her throat. She wanted him to be hard and clumsy, or wet and unpleasant, but his mouth was warm and dry as it met hers, and there was a subtle mastery in his kiss that dragged the soul from her body. Instinct warned her of his sophistication; innocence recognised the perils of addiction, but her untutored body ignored all the warnings, and she sighed as a sensation so exquisite it was almost pain shot through her.

Unlike most other men who had kissed her he didn't try to drag her close, forcing her to acknowledge exactly what he wanted of her. His grip was firm, but not constricting; she felt protected and cherished, not ravished. Either he intuitively knew how to deal with any woman, or he was extremely experienced. She wanted more, drawn by the dark tides stirring in her blood to flirt with the danger she sensed in him.

In a voice she realised was shaking, he whispered, 'Kathy?'

His breath on her lips was almost as erotic as the kiss had been. The thick fans of her lashes lifted, and she stared up at him with a dazed, languid yearning. On a muffled groan he dragged her closer, his mouth crushing hers as though he were dying for her, his whole being intent only on that kiss. It was intoxicating; she felt as high on passion as on good French champagne, passion and the knowledge that she could do this to this man, this incredibly attractive man.

And then any coherent thought was gone, swamped by a flood of sensations so intense that she moaned a surrender, lost in the compelling demands of a hunger like nothing she had ever experienced before.

It could have been hours later when she surfaced, her mouth trembling, her body pressed with a total lack of restraint against the taut contours of his. He desired her, and far from being repelled she fed on his passion, aching with need, wanting only one thing—to discover at last the secrets her innate fastidiousness had postponed until then.

As he eased her away he said softly, amusement and need interweaving in the deep textures of his voice, 'Did I say dangerous? Bloody terrifying would describe it better. But not here, Kathy. Not here.'

She should have been racked with shame, but some singing part of her knew that there was no place for shame in this. However, as if to underline his words, an aggrieved voice from behind him said, 'So that's where you've got to, Kathy. Do you still want this drink, or are you too busy?'

'She's too busy,' André Hunter said succinctly.

Martin peered around the broad shoulder blocking his way. He looked smaller and far less confident than he had when they danced together. After one good look at Kathy's face he shrugged and said acidly, 'Oh, well, you might as well have the drink. Perhaps we'll have another dance later on, Kathy.'

Kathy's answer was forestalled. 'No,' André Hunter said simply, but there was enough arrogant possession in the syllable to make Martin shrug again as he put the glass on the edge of the wide rail.

'OK,' he said, striving and almost succeeding to make his voice casual.

Neither noticed his offended departure. Kathy was torn between pleasure at André's obvious hunger for her company, and anger at him for being so brutally laconic to poor Martin. She solved the problem by taking the lime juice and drinking it slowly, turning away a little while striving to come to terms with what was happening to her.

André said quietly, 'Trying to rationalise it won't get rid of it, Kathy. It's there, like a force of nature. In fact, it is a force of nature.'

In spite of herself, she couldn't stop the startled look she sent him. He was too damned perceptive by half. 'Why are you called André?' she asked. 'It's an unusual name.'

If he was surprised at the abrupt change of subject he didn't show it. 'My mother was French.'

Which explained the deep copper skin and the dark hair, although not the red highlights that gleamed in it. She nodded, remembering now where she had seen his name. Using his father's industrial empire as a base, he had made what he casually referred to as a hobby of taking over rundown and derelict businesses and reviving them. One journalist had described him as an entrepreneur with a conscience, adding cynically that this was so unusual it seemed only fair that most of his projects had come back with a bang from the dead and were now nicely profitable.

At the age of twenty-six, André Hunter was already a seasoned businessman, and on the way to being a very rich one. All of which was interesting, and a possible reason for the effortless air of command that marked him out from other men, but it didn't explain the swash-buckling aura that surrounded him, a kind of wicked charm that drew women powerfully. He had figured in the gossip pages as well as the financial ones; Kathy recognised that potent attraction even as she realised its capacity for harm.

'And who exactly are you?' he said lazily, although the words were an order. 'Tell me all about yourself.'

'There's not much to tell.'

'How old are you?'

'Eighteen.'

'A baby,' he mocked, watching her with those devilish green eyes. 'And local, clearly.'

'No, I'm not really local, although I live in Auckland now. I was born in Southland.'

'What brought you up to the North Island? It's a long long way from home.'

She hesitated. Did she really want to explain the reason she had come to Auckland? Her teeth chewed on her full lower lip, but finally, under that unnerving, unwinking regard, she temporised by saying, 'I came up because I have—had—a cousin here, and he offered me a place to live while I went to university.'

'Had a cousin?'

She drank a little more of the sweet-sour lime juice, giving her wild confusion of emotions time to settle down. Little chills of sensation still iced through her veins, but her voice was steady as she told him, 'He's no longer in Auckland. He's a scientist; he's doing a stint on Raoul Island in the Kermadecs.'

'I see.' His tone was cool, almost abstracted, and she felt a chill of a different sort. 'You are fond of him?'

'I love him very dearly,' she said simply.

Married late, her parents had never been able to understand their daughter; conventional, old-fashioned, they had wanted her to stay in the small town where she had grown up, marry a nice steady boy and settle down to give them grandchildren. To this end they had actively discouraged her from any thoughts of higher education.

Ambitious, aware that she would stultify in the sort of life they had found so satisfactory, Kathy had fled as soon as she could to Chris, like her a refugee from a stifling existence centred on the family farm. They had flatted together in Auckland, and the last year had been idyllic—until Olivia Saywell, the woman Chris loved, had killed herself.

Stop, Kathy adjured herself. It's no use, it's over, it's done with. Olivia is dead and Chris is in hell, stuck on Raoul Island with his scientific expedition in a sort of guilt-induced expiation for sins he didn't commit.

Both he and she would suffer from their consciences for the rest of their lives. But they had not, she thought savagely as she remembered Olivia's screaming viciousness the last time she had seen her, suffered as much as Olivia, from the accident that took from her all that she valued: her slender grace, her vitality, but most of all her seductive beauty and its power over men.

'What is it?' André Hunter asked sharply. 'What is the matter?'

She looked up vaguely, her eyes slowly focusing on his dark hawkish features. 'I—nothing,' she lied.

He smiled at that, a hint of mockery replacing the concern. 'I don't like it when you go away from me like that. Come and dance.'

But when they got inside again he looked around the crowded room with distaste. 'Not here,' he said, apparently supremely unaware of the glances that followed them, interested envious glances that were avid with speculation. Looking down, he lifted a winged brow. 'Somewhere quieter, I think.'

She returned a very direct look. 'Where, exactly?'

'My place? No? Then how about a drink somewhere? And after that I'll take you home, I promise.'

She hesitated, torn between caution and her instinctive response to the challenge that glittered in his glance, the cynical little smile that pulled at the corners of his beautifully cut mouth. But it was not a thoughtless response to a dare that made her nod swiftly, almost recklessly. Curiosity ate at her; she wanted to know all about him, to discover the lights and shadows of his personality. A primal need to understand him as well as she did herself compelled her acquiescence.

'But I'd better tell my flatmate,' she said, 'She can be a bit mother-hennish sometimes.' And she had this strange idea that Kathy was an innocent newly up from the country.

Refusing to be embarrassed by his raised brows, she looked about, striving to catch sight of Libby's glowing golden head with its wild frizz of curls.

'What does she look like?'

'Tall and very attractive—ah, there she is, over by the door.'

'Right.'

This time he took the lead, effortlessly cleaving a path through the crowd, holding her hand clasped firmly in the warm strength of his. Easy when you're tall, she thought, trying very hard to summon some sort of objectivity to the situation. Like a nurse she monitored her body's signs, wondering at the strange pull that set her heart beating double time, made her feel preternaturally alert so that the music seemed to well up from inside her bones, stretched already taut skin, honed hearing and sight to the point of pain.

Was it the same for him? Yes, she thought, remembering with the greedy joy of a miser snatching a gold coin how his face had been drawn and stark with a primitive, basic emotion when he kissed her. Yes, he felt it too, that mindless urgency.

To say that Libby was startled at her decision to leave with André Hunter would be an exaggeration; she did not normally allow much emotion to mark her features. However, her brows shot up when she looked from the dark saturnine face of the man who towered above her to Kathy's, shy yet somehow secretive. 'OK,' she said cheerfully. 'Thanks for letting me know. I'll expect you when I see you.'

Once outside the house André asked sardonically, 'Do you always have to report to her?'

'No.' Her voice was cool and dismissive. 'If either one of us decides to leave a party sooner than the other we let each other know.' She flashed him a somewhat narrowed look. 'Women tend to do that sort of thing,' she finished sweetly. 'It can be a dangerous world.'

He nodded, the corners of his mouth tucking into a wry smile. 'Point taken. But I'm sure I detected a faint admonitory tinge to her attitude.'

'In spite of her spectacular looks,' Kathy admitted, 'she has a strong maternal streak.'

'How long have you flatted with her?'

'Three weeks.' Those eyebrows winged up in a mephistophelean fashion and she went on, 'I lived with my cousin until he decided to go to the Kermadecs but when he left I couldn't afford the rent. Libby is an old friend of Chris's and she had to move from her old place, so it made sense for her to come in with me. We needed a third, so we advertised and that's how Fiona joined us.'

'And you all get on well together?'

The cynicism in his tone made her bristle. 'Yes, we do, very well.'

'When is your cousin coming back?'

She sighed softly. 'In a year, unless he decides to stay on longer.'

Stopping by a long, low black car, André unlocked the passenger door, putting her in with a courtesy that was as natural and inbuilt as his cool air of sophistication. The French mother? Kathy watched him stride to the driver's side, his body all clean long lines in the light of a street lamp, his gait a smooth predator's pace, easy and relaxed. Yet there was, she sensed, some hint of tension in him somewhere. Perhaps it was the same alert wariness that imprisoned her in its grip.

'What,' he asked casually as he fitted the key into the slot, 'is he doing on Raoul Island? Is he a meteorologist?'

It was a reasonable assumption. The island was one of a chain of volcanic peaks far to the north of New Zealand, uninhabited except for the weather-men who lived at the lonely tropical station for a year at a time.

'No, he's not. He's doing a study on the Greenhouse Effect.'

'Interesting.' The key turned, the engine sprang throatily into life. 'A year is quite a chunk out of his life.'

She could have told him that Chris was sick at heart, that the woman he loved had committed suicide because she hadn't been able to face the thought of life confined to a wheelchair, but she didn't. Chris's purgatory was his alone, shared to a lesser extent by her.

And Chris had suffered more than she had. For he had truly loved Olivia, whose cruelty had increased with her pain. Made vicious by pain and despair, she had done her best to strip him of his manhood. Yet Chris had visited her every day at the hospital until at last she told him she never wanted to see him again.

A bitter ache closed Kathy's throat as she stared out of the window at the warm darkness. He had been shattered, refusing to accept her edict. The next day he had gone again to the hospital, and been politely but firmly turned away. Olivia had barred him.

It was so unfair, because Olivia had caused the accident. They had all been coming back from a party up the coast, Kathy at the wheel, Chris dozing in the back because he had taken hayfever medication that prohibited driving. High on some hellish cocktail of alcohol and drugs, Olivia had refused to put on a safety-belt until forced into it by an angry and distressed Chris, helped by Libby who was spending the night with her brother, their host.

It had been wet so Kathy had had to concentrate hard all the way along the narrow coastal road. They would have made it without incident, only Olivia had woken and grabbed the wheel during a screaming frantic quarrel; the car had run off the road over a cliff, the doors spilling open. Strapped in, Chris and Kathy had suffered only minor injuries, but some time during the journey Olivia had freed herself from the constraints of the seatbelt. She had been thrown on to the unforgiving rocks below. Her injuries had been horrific, and when she had learned that she would never walk again, never dance and love again, never enslave another man with the allure of her lithe sensuous body, she had saved up every sedative and tranquilliser and pain-killer she could lay hands on, and this time the cocktail of drugs had killed her.

It was then that Chris had applied for the post on Raoul.

'Yes,' Kathy said softly, 'it's a big chunk out of anyone's life.'

'He must be dedicated. Or is he perhaps hiding from something?'

Her head swung. Against the lights of the North Shore his profile was a strong statement, an autocratic line of nose and chin, the firm moulding of lips that had been warm and sweet on hers. Something moved in the pit of her stomach. She asked harshly, 'What on earth do you mean?'

His shoulders moved a little. 'Nothing, merely that often people who volunteer to go into exile hope that the time away will result in healing.'

Slowly she relaxed. 'Perhaps you're right.'

'Or, possibly, it's not healing they need, but a refuge.'

A sanctuary where time could work its spell. Chris had loved Olivia with a strength that had awed Kathy, and the resultant disillusion had been shattering, stripping him of confidence. Yes, Chris needed a refuge.

'Could be,' she said quietly. Then, because she didn't want this evening to be spoilt by thoughts of her cousin's tragedy, she asked, 'Where are we going?'

'A pub.'

The pub turned out to be a very up-market bar in a city hotel, newly refurbished and decorated in a subtle modern way that managed to be both trendy and in keeping with the old building. Gazing around in some awe, Kathy recognised faces she had only seen in newspapers and glossy magazines. She must, she realised with an odd pang, seem very ordinary compared to most of the *habitués*.

André steered her to a small table in a dimly lit corner, and seated her. A waitress was already approaching.

'Champagne,' he said, ordering a famous French brand.

Kathy's brows climbed, but she said nothing.

'I think we should celebrate,' he said, looking at her with unmistakable pleasure, his voice very deep and low. 'Tonight is an auspicious occasion.'

They sat there until at last the bar manager flicked the lights at them; Kathy felt drunk, although neither had finished the first glass. They had talked long and earnestly, the quiet, intense conversation broken by moments when both had laughed.

It was amazing how much they shared: the same sense of humour, and the same interests in music and art and literature; even a few hobbies, the theatre and going for long walks in lonely country. He enjoyed fast cars, which made her shudder, and heli-skiing, which she had never done, although she had spent holidays with relatives in the snow country and was an expert on skis. They thought alike on many issues, argued pleasurably and without heat on others, discussed much with an absorbed concentration she had never experienced before.

Walking back to the car with his hand at her elbow, she realised that she was drunk on his presence, floating three feet above the ground, her blood fizzing through her veins, heart and mind animated as never before.

Back in those incredibly comfortable seats he said, 'Home?'

'Yes,' she said, sighing, some of the delicious anticipation subsiding, because of course they had to go home even though it wasn't very late. She gave him her address and he smiled and set the powerful beast in motion, his lean, tanned hands skilled on the wheel.

Auckland was an enchanted city, its lights transfigured into fairy lanterns, its streets to magical highways leading to some unknown, fabled land of pleasure.

I think I'm falling in love, she thought, a part of her terrified at the prospect, but mostly saturated by a sense of rightness as though this had been destined since the beginning of time. Outside the large house that had been divided into five flats she asked shyly, 'Would you like to come in for coffee?'

'Yes.'

Prickles of delight ran through her. Frantically she tried to remember how she had left the place, then gave up. She didn't care; it wasn't of any importance.

However it was tidy, and Fiona, the other member of the trio, was not yet back from the concert she was attending. Kathy put on the kettle and measured the coffee into the plunge percolator, then set out the cups, not looking his way but seeing from the corner of her eyes the way he stood in the centre of the room and looked around it, measuring it, his lids dropped over those incredible eyes so that she couldn't see what he was thinking.

He was absolutely stunning to look at, she thought. Not conventionally handsome; something more, something that would pass the test of time. Radiating a kind of sensual charisma that caught the eye effortlessly, backed as it was by a perfect body and those striking features, he looked like a handsome bandit. Yet it was not just his physical attributes that impinged so strongly on her. His intelligence had impressed her too, that sharp, subtle brain with its keen understanding of the human condition. Add this to a bone-deep confidence that came within a hair's breadth of arrogance, and the aura of competence that so few men could lay claim to, and he was a fabulous male.

And she asked herself the obvious. What was such a fabulous man doing with her? Oh, she was attractive enough, if without distinction; she was reasonably intelligent, she could move well when she was dancing. And that was all. At eighteen she was almost pitifully unsophisticated, whereas André Hunter looked as though he had been born worldly.

So what did he see in her? Alpha men normally went for Alpha women, and she knew what they were like. Beautiful, with a feminine appeal that matched that of the men they attracted. Not impecunious university undergraduates, unworldly and socially inexperienced.

The kettle boiled and she poured the water into the percolator, then emerged from behind the bar, a sudden acute shyness gripping her.

He had walked across to the window and was staring out at the lights of the city, sprinkled like a carpet of stardust beneath them. The flat was on the upper storey of the house, which was tucked above the level of the rest of Auckland on one of the small volcanoes that made it unlike any other city in the world.

'Fantastic view,' he murmured in that deep, fascinating voice.

'Yes, isn't it?'

He knew how she was feeling. His half-mocking, half-understanding smile told her.

'Second thoughts?' he murmured as he reached for her. 'It's too late, Kathy. I don't know what the hell this is, but we'd be cowards if we didn't find out.'

His mouth was warm and persuasive, subtly coercive as though he was afraid that she would send him away. It gave her a fleeting sense of power that was gone almost as soon as it came, swamped by the clamour of desire that overrode everything else: common sense, pragmatism, the everyday wisdom by which she had lived her life until that evening.

'Are you a coward?' His voice was shaken, almost rough with tension.

'Yes, but——'

He kissed along her eyelids, sending erotic little thrills through her nerves. 'No buts,' he murmured. 'Don't give me boring objections, Kathy. I don't think this has anything to do with common sense. I've never felt like this before. Have you?'

'You know I haven't,' she said, shivering. She knew about sex—it was almost impossible to pick up a magazine without reading an article on it. Why had she never understood that a man's breath in her ear, his teeth closing so gently on the soft lobe, could send her heart rate soaring up into the stratosphere?

'Coffee,' she said, the word coming thickly off her tongue.

He laughed. 'To hell with coffee,' he muttered as his mouth searched for and found hers.

It seemed hours later that finally she was able to pull away, her face flushed, her body singing with an aching frustration. 'No,' she gasped. 'No, André. No.'

He was breathing raggedly, his cheekbones stark, his shadowed eyelids hiding all but blazing slivers of green, and she felt his resistance to her plea with every particle of her being. But after a moment's crystalline stare at her trembling, slightly swollen mouth and dilated, pleading eyes, he nodded, and released her, stepping back as she fumbled the strap of her bodysuit straight and drew a deep shaking breath.

'I'll go,' he said unevenly.

She shook her head. 'The coffee...'

'If I stay I'm going to finish up in your bed,' he said, watching her with an oblique, unsettling intensity that sent warning signals dancing through her.

Colour fired her skin again. Rebellion screamed inside her, a fierce need that stabbed her with intolerable sensations, a deep-seated ache for completion, but she knew it was too soon. She hesitated, then gave him an apologetic look. 'You had better go, then.'

'I'll call you tomorrow morning,' he said, smiling that blade-edged smile again. 'Goodnight, Kathy.'

'Goodnight.'

She followed him across and locked the door, then dreamily turned off the lights and drifted across to the window so that she could see down to the driveway. The glass was cool against her forehead; her breath made a little patch of condensation on it. She held her breath as he strode out of the building and across the footpath. He looked like a modern god, she thought dizzily, another clutch of desire hurting her with its intensity.

Just before he got into the car he lifted his hand in an ironic salute. Kathy felt like a voyeur; she could have wailed her embarrassment to the silent night.

CHAPTER TWO

'ALL right,' Libby said, fixing an embarrassed Kathy with a gimlet eye. 'Tell all.'

'There's nothing to tell. We met at the party, we went to the Nouveau bar at the Criterion and had a drink, we came home and I made some coffee, and then he left and I went to bed. Well before three o'clock, which was when you got home!'

'It was a good party.' Libby dismissed this weak attempt to change the subject with the contempt it deserved. 'And I've no doubt that that is roughly what happened. What I'd like to know is how you walked out of the room with the man who is not only the most eligible bachelor in Auckland but the most notorious.'

'Do you know him?'

'No, but I know of him. Everyone does. And I had only to look at him to see that the stories are all true; he is utterly fascinating and wicked and exciting. The man strides around immersed in a devilish aura, fairly seething with spine-tingling possibilities.'

'Too devilish for me?' Well, it was only what she had thought herself, heaven knew.

Libby's expression softened. Gracefully lowering herself into a dining chair, she leaned forward, fixing Kathy with a sapient stare as she used her toast to emphasise her point. 'Dear girl, in spite of your valiant efforts to achieve worldliness, you haven't got there yet. Of course the man wants you; hell, when you dance you look like the answer to any lecher's prayers. But you know and I know that you're not the hot little number

25

you seem to be when the music starts getting into your bones. What's worrying me is whether he knows it!'

'He should,' Kathy returned spiritedly. 'We did an awful lot of talking.'

The older woman eyed her dubiously but accepted the unspoken reproach. 'OK,' she said. 'You do know, don't you, that he was Olivia Saywell's lover?'

The colour drained from Kathy's skin so suddenly that Libby leapt to her feet. 'Sit down,' she said urgently, not reseating herself until Kathy was safely in the chair. 'No, you didn't know.'

'When was that?'

Libby shrugged. 'Of course, Olivia was a liar. You know how she used to tease and torment Chris just to take the edge off her boredom? Well, one day I overheard her telling him that he was the best lover she had ever had. André, I mean, not poor old Chris.'

Kathy had her suspicions about Libby's feelings for her cousin, suspicions she kept very firmly to herself. Nausea gripped her, the same sickness she used to feel when Olivia was being feline, but after a moment she said stoutly, 'I'm not going to let that upset me.' Her mouth twisted. 'After all, Chris was her lover too, and I don't think any the less of him for it.'

Libby began to say something, but changed her mind. 'So, when do you see the sexy André Hunter again?'

'I don't know.'

'And what about Brent?'

Kathy stared at her. A free-lance writer, Brent Sheridan owned the lawnmowing business at which she worked in her spare hours. He had been exceptionally kind to her, even passing Chris's stern standards for an escort, although her cousin had cavilled at his age, which was almost thirty. They had gone out together several times, but beyond a pleasant kiss at the end of the evening he had shown no signs of wanting to deepen the relationship.

'What about Brent?' she asked, startled.

Libby sighed and rolled her eyes. 'For heaven's sake, you really have just come out of the egg. The man's in love with you.'

'*Brent?* Oh, Lib, don't be silly. Brent's a dear, but he's never shown any signs of being——'

'He's taken you out, hasn't he? A man doesn't take a woman out if he's not interested. And he's no callow youth, so keen to get you into bed that he forces the issue. The man knows how to wait.'

'Come on, Lib, stop mothering her.' Fiona yawned her way out from the kitchen, cup of coffee in her hand. 'In spite of those huge soulful innocent eyes, she's a big girl now. If the man is as gorgeous as you'd have us believe, then you go to it, Kathy. They don't come along often, and when they do, I say enjoy them. And if he ends up breaking your heart, well, hearts mend and every woman needs a tragic love-affair in her past.'

'This,' Libby said cheerfully, 'from Miss Love-Them-And-Leave-Them herself! All right, I hereby resign from the honorary and thankless position of den mother, and promise never to suggest again that you might not be able to deal with Casanova himself if he came on the scene.'

The telephone rang. Fiona reached out and said, 'Yes?' Silence, then she smiled and in a different voice said, 'Yes, she's here, Mr Hunter. I'll get her for you.'

It was difficult to talk even though both Libby and Fiona moved out of hearing range. Kathy's voice was shy when she said, 'Hello.'

'Hello.' There was laughter in his tone. 'Would you like to go for a picnic today?'

'Love to.'

'Good. I'll pick you up in half an hour.'

He had hung up before she could ask him where they were going, and whether she should bring food.

'Well?' Libby had forgotten her vow of only a few minutes ago and was eyeing her like a hen whose single chick was about to be snatched away. Fiona also looked sleepily interested.

'We're going for a picnic,' Kathy said with as much dignity as she could muster, heading out of the room before they could catechise her any further.

She was ready within the half-hour, dressed in an oversized oyster T-shirt and a short, full cinnamon divided skirt. Her mane of hair was subdued into neatness and tied with a scarf in cinnamon and oyster and gold, and over it she wore a large straw hat. Buckling a narrow belt over the wide waistband of the skirt, she came through into the sitting-room, but her fingers stopped as she stared around in surprise. Instead of the usual pleasant clutter of Sunday morning the room was neat and tidy, and Fiona was out on the veranda pretending not to peer over the balustrade.

'Very nice,' Libby said, dishcloth in hand, as she emerged from the kitchen. 'You look delicious enough to eat. I envy you being able to sew, it must save you a packet.'

Kathy shrugged. 'My mother thinks every woman should know how to sew and knit, and cook, and keep house. But she doesn't think that managing your own finances is important. That's a man's job.' In spite of herself she couldn't prevent the note of bitterness that roughened her voice.

'She grew up in a different era.'

'I know, but there's no reason why she should stay in it.'

'Well, I wish my mother had taught me how to sew as well as you do.'

'Buy some material, and I'll make you whatever you like.'

Libby regarded her with intensified respect. 'Can you draft patterns yourself?'

'Yes, it's quite easy when you know how.'

'Oh, yes, and so's splitting the atom, I'm sure. Well, if you do, I'll pay you——'

'What ho within!' Fiona hissed through the open french windows. 'A sleek black Panthera has just driven up, and getting out of it is the most gorgeous male I have ever seen.' There followed a startled gurgle and she slid inside, flushed and laughing. 'He's also got damned good hearing. He looked up and waved.'

Perhaps it was his usual habit when arriving and leaving, the casual wave towards the window. Kathy swallowed, wondering if the magic had suddenly died overnight. Had he really been Olivia's lover, or had she just been playing one of her cruel little games?

And—would it make any difference to Kathy if he had been?

But when she met him at the door it was still there, strong and sweet and alarming, that tumultuous tugging of the senses that had made her dreams so chaotic. He felt it, too. He didn't make any attempt to kiss her, but his smile was intimate and his eyes roved across the soft coral of her mouth with a knowing intensity that brought swift colour to her cheeks.

'Ready?' he asked in a deep voice.

She nodded. 'You already know Libby, but come in and meet Fiona,' she invited.

He was charm itself, those olive eyes acknowledging her flatmate's voluptuous contours with a worldly appreciation that grated a little. Fiona clearly returned his admiration but, as she was not the sort who flirted with another woman's man, she toned down her usual insouciant coquettishness. Nevertheless, Kathy was pleased when she was finally tucked up in the Panthera.

'Your friends don't think I'm going to be a good influence on you,' he remarked as he backed out on to the quiet leafy street.

'Oh, no, Fiona said——' The words were out before she had time to think. Heat crawled across her skin as she realised she had given Libby away.

His soft chuckle was amused yet there was a note of mockery in it that increased her blush. 'Oh, yes. They're both thoroughly nice women, and that means they're protective of someone they consider to be an innocent.'

She groaned. 'I don't know why. I've been in Auckland for a year—plenty of time to get into trouble if I were that sort!'

'A whole year,' he teased, 'and with a cousin riding shotgun for most of that! What degree are you aiming for, Kathy?'

'English.'

'Ah. Do you intend to teach?'

'No,' she said quietly. Her gaze fell. Sometimes her lack of ideas for any future career worried her.

'No?'

She cast a quick nervous look up at his profile, found her eyes lingering on the beautiful curves of the mouth that could wring such incredible sensations from her. He slanted an enigmatic look her way.

Baldly she said, 'I still have a couple of years to make up my mind what I want to do.' The sight of his lean brown hands moving competently on the wheel caused an odd little shudder in the pit of her stomach.

His voice was uninflected as he asked, 'Are you taking any other papers besides English ones?'

She laughed. 'A couple of Anthropology units, some Political Studies, Art History—as much as I can fit in without spoiling my chances of getting an English degree.'

'Why did you choose Auckland? If you come from Southland, Dunedin would have been closer to home. Don't your parents miss you?'

That unconscious bitterness edged her tone. 'My parents are firmly rooted in the past. They don't think a woman needs a degree, because she's only going to get married, and that's taking a place from a man who needs it to support a family.'

'Good God. I thought that sort of outlook had died twenty-five years ago.'

'Nope. I was the only girl at school whose parents refused to help her beyond School Certificate.'

He slanted her another glance. 'They wanted you to stay home?'

She grimaced. 'Oh, very much so. They decided that if I really wanted to go to university it would have to be under my own steam.'

'What about your brothers and sisters?' he asked gently.

She sighed. 'There aren't any.'

'Then perhaps it's understandable that they want you close to them.'

'Yes, I can appreciate that, but they—they're so narrow! They wanted me to leave after the sixth form; I had to fight to go back for a seventh form year, then they wouldn't pay for me to sit Bursary and Scholarship. I did that myself with money I'd saved up. My mother thinks that reading is a waste of time. When I was a kid I was allowed one library book a week. And I had to do all sorts of chores before I was allowed to read it.'

'I'm sure it didn't do you any harm.'

She smiled reluctantly. 'No, I don't suppose it did, but sometimes I used to wonder if I was a foundling! We have such diametrically opposed viewpoints on everything. I think they hoped that if they didn't help me at university I'd come crawling back home with my tail between my legs, but I'd rather die!' Her chin, with its intriguing cleft, jutted with a proud determination that somehow managed to make her look very young.

'I suppose they wonder what they've given birth to,' he mused. 'A colourful little peacock in their sedate sparrow's nest. It's called the generation gap, and it happens all the time, Kathy.'

'I know it does, but—oh, they wouldn't even try to understand.' She sighed and turned her head to the side. 'I love them, and in their way they love me, too, but they won't accept that my ways of doing things are right for me. I honestly think I might have gone mad or bad, or both, if it hadn't been for Chris!'

There was a small strained silence. She was just beginning to glance curiously at him when he spoke. 'Growing up can be a painful process for everyone involved, but they'll probably come around in time,' he said, as he swung the car into the car park of a large marina on the Tamaki river.

'André,' she said tentatively, 'who are we going out with?'

'Just us,' he said, his smile spiced with a hint of challenge. 'Afraid?'

She reacted with a surging recklessness that lent glittering lights to her gaze. 'No,' she said coolly. 'Should I be?'

'Let's see, shall we?'

His boat was a medium-size cruiser, but its luxury was startling, almost oppressive. Still, she admired it lavishly, watching with interest as he took it carefully out through the rows and rows of boats, visible evidence of Auckland's love-affair with the beautiful Hauraki Gulf, playground for the city.

As she had known he would be, he was skilful, keeping to the five-knot speed limit as they went down the sparkling river. Even here there was enough breeze to combat the humidity; she enjoyed the feeling of her hair lifting in the wind, a tangle of dark copper about her shoulders. Her eyes sparkled gold and amber in the delicate wind-kissed contours of her face. Bubbles of excitement fizzed through her, colouring the world in champagne hues.

'Where are we going?' she asked.

He pointed across the harbour. 'See the island behind Waiheke? The little one?'

'Yes.'

'Well, it belongs to a woman I went to primary school with. She's overseas at the moment, and we're going to land on it and have a picnic.'

She smiled with brilliant delight. 'I've never been on an island,' she confessed.

He looked startled. 'Really? Have you been out on the harbour?'

'No. I've been working too hard, and Chris is not a water person.'

His smile looked more as though he bared his teeth, but he merely said mildly, 'He'll be seeing enough of it where he is now! So today is the first time you've been out on the gulf? Well, you can't call yourself an Aucklander until you've sailed. It's *de rigueur*!'

It was a day of unalloyed delight. Looking back on it, Kathy thought she had never been so happy, so innocently self-centred, basking in his unadulterated attention, her skin slowly gilding in the slow heat under a brilliant sky, while André showed her the myriad hues of the sea and the land, from the smooth peaks of the looming Hunua hills to the south to the more distant Coromandel ranges on the other side of the Firth of Thames.

'One day,' she said, when André had pointed these last out, 'I'm going there. I've always wanted to see the Coromandel. It sounds—apart, somehow. Different.'

'It's different enough, if by that you mean exquisitely beautiful. It's a fascinating place, with some fantastic beaches and superb scenery. Lots of relics of the gold-mining days, some magnificent views and areas of bush. Kauri trees grow there as well as they do in Northland. I'll take you there one day.'

He seemed to know about everything. He named all the islands that dotted the gulf, from the most obvious, the dormant volcano Rangitoto, to the largest in area, Waiheke; he took her past Motuaroha, where the famous Caird family had lived until the latest one moved to the mainland.

'Oh,' she breathed, transfixed by the exquisite Greek revival mansion she could just see through magnificent pohutukawa trees. 'Why did they sell it?'

He laughed, somewhat cynically. 'He's a Caird, Kathy. He didn't sell it, he didn't need to. It's still his, but he married a doctor, and as she couldn't practise on the island he bought land on the mainland. That's where they live now, about halfway to Whangarei. She's the local doctor, and he's enjoying himself bringing a long-neglected station back into production.'

There was an odd note in his voice that persuaded her to guess, 'Would you like to do that?'

'What?'

'Bring neglected land back into production.'

A short silence and he said, 'Yes, I suppose I would. It would give me great satisfaction to create something from nothing.'

So that was why he liked to take over derelict companies and coax them into profitability. He had given her a small glimpse of the man beneath the glittering sensual charisma. She stowed it away in her memory like a small jewel, allowing herself to ponder a little wistfully on the strength of a love that had persuaded the last Caird to give up an island that looked like the last step before paradise.

A swift glance at André revealed that he was watching her, smiling a little. 'A romantic story, isn't it?' he said a little derisively. 'Yet I'd say that Blake Caird is possibly the least romantic man I've ever met.'

'Yes, I think it is,' she said sturdily. 'Perhaps falling in love changed his outlook.'

He sent her a grave, unsmiling look. 'I knew you were a romantic the moment I saw you. You danced with a kind of sensual abandon that was totally unconscious. And when I looked into your eyes, I was convinced. Eyes like that have to belong to someone passionate and emotional.'

The way he lingered over the words made her skin prickle but she lifted her eyes in mock resentment. 'You make me sound a drip,' she said briskly. 'A slave to my feelings!'

'Oh, no.' His gaze roved the contours of her face, setting off little fires in her sensitised skin. 'Your character is in your face, Kathy. There's toughness there too, and courage, and determination.'

Infuriatingly her ready colour proved her embarrassment. He laughed softly and bent to kiss her mouth. 'And when you blush you look like a ripe apricot,' he murmured. 'Soft and sweet and delicious, with enough of a tang to avoid cloying.'

It was just as well that they came out of the lee of an island and into a short brisk chop where he had to concentrate, for Kathy had no defence against the languid tide of desire that floated through every cell in her body. Buoyed by it, she looked eagerly ahead to the little island that was their destination.

As its name indicated, Motuiti was small, but much of it was farmed. However, the beach to which André guided them was backed by bush, shadowed and still, pulsating with cicadas, the tall crowns of tariare trees pushing above the rest of the coastal forest. He pulled into a small cove where the sand lay blindingly white beneath the sun. In spite of the hundreds of yachts and motorboats they had seen on their way, the beach and little bay were deserted.

The big cruiser was shallow enough in the water to take them almost to the beach, but for the last fifty metres they had to use the rubber dinghy. Together they packed several baskets and boxes into it, then set off for the shore.

'We'd better put the food in the shade of that big pohutukawa,' André said as he cut the engine. 'Spread the rug out, will you? I'll bring up the rest.'

Sandals in one hand, Kathy splashed through the warm ankle-deep water and carried the rug across already sizzling sand to the welcome coolness of the shade beneath the huge limbs of the tree. The rug was large and not new, and although spotlessly clean somehow had an aura of other picnics, other days spent in sybaritic laziness beside the sea. As she spread it she watched André's lean figure come towards her. Had he taken other women out on days like this, used this rug, this bay even? Olivia Saywell, perhaps?

Of course he had, she told herself bleakly. If not Olivia, there were bound to have been others. He was sophisticated and attractive; she had seen women's eyes on him last night, speculative, assessing, compulsively interested. There must have been plenty of women in his life.

Falling in love with André Hunter would be about the most stupid, dangerous, useless thing she could do. It would be tantamount to lying down in front of a locomotive, stepping off a cliff, cuddling a tiger. All three at once, she thought, made a little hysterical by the sudden attack of common sense warring with unbidden, as yet unformed dreams.

OK, so he looked like the world's most handsome eagle, and he was wrapped in an aura of dangerous masculinity that set her senses tingling, but the key word was *dangerous*, and she had better things to do with her life than try to mend a broken heart.

Then he looked down at her and her doubts and worries died in the blazing caress of his eyes. He felt something for her. What might come of it she didn't know, but she wasn't going to let fear and her lack of confidence stop her from finding out.

The enchantment continued. They swam, she neat and provocative in her toffee-coloured maillot, he striking in moss-green racing briefs that emphasised the deep silken copper of his skin. Tension sizzled and simmered between them, but he made no move to touch her, and she too kept her distance. It was as though they were playing a game, she thought, feasting her eyes on the sleek musculature of his body, perfectly proportioned, perfectly balanced; a game where the rules were set to prolong and enhance the excitement.

She ate lunch with delicate greed: cold duck and a delicious array of salads; crusty wholemeal bread; an assortment of fruit, brilliant ruby tamarillos with their sweet/tart taste and incomparable flavour, sweet green kiwi fruit, glowing oranges and mandarins; and several cheeses to go with them, including her favourite, a tangy blue-vein.

'I thought young palates didn't like this,' he observed lazily, spreading some on a cracker and holding it up to her mouth, his eyes gleaming.

Confused, she took a mouthful, chewing without taste as he ate the rest. It seemed a profoundly erotic thing to do, yet she didn't know why. Perhaps it was his clean, salty masculine scent, or the fact that her heart sped up whenever he came close. She looked down at her arms, noting with dismay the tiny prickle of goose-flesh across her satin skin. He was the first man to have such a physical effect on her, and although she thrilled to his presence she was too much her mother's daughter to be at ease with what was happening.

'I've always liked cheese with a bit of bite,' she said, hastily buttering another cracker.

Her gaze strayed sideways; he was leaning back against one of the branches of the tree, watching her with a mesmeric little smile tugging at his chiselled mouth.

Responding to the provocation of that smile with a swift challenge of her own, she held out the biscuit, and when his strong white teeth had crunched into it she picked up a cluster of cool green grapes and fed them to him, one by one.

His lashes drooped but behind the thick screen she could see the gleam of his eyes, alert yet oddly detached. Like him, she had pulled her T-shirt over her bathing suit and was sitting back on her heels, her face absorbed as she fed him the grapes. At first she made sure that her fingers stayed well away from his lips, but as she gained confidence she grew slower to pull away, until with the last grape he took the tip of her finger into his warm mouth and delicately, subversively, bit it.

Her breath died in her throat. She must have made a soft little gasping noise because he smiled very slowly and reached out to pull her into his arms as his mouth teased hers, kissing the corners, along the full, passionate length, searching for the elusive dimple that trembled beside it, and finally, the cleft in her chin.

'*Tu m'enivres!*' he said thickly, against her lips. 'You make me drunk. Just the sight of you, golden and tangy as the best wine, clear and sparkling and transparent.'

As his heart picked up speed against hers, she shuddered and sighed into his mouth, made her own tentative demands, touching a series of fugitive kisses to the sculptured outline of his lips, the faint rasp of his beard a magnificent seductive contrast to the oiled silk of his skin.

She thought she whispered his name as slowly, shyly, she deepened the kiss. His arms tightened and he made a soft throaty sound, but he made no attempt to take over, allowing her the freedom to explore. She took it with a kind of greedy innocence, her shyness fading, becoming transmuted into the open need to touch him.

Her mouth found the high stark sweep of his cheekbones, the surprisingly soft length of his lashes, the smooth wide expanse of forehead. She kissed along his jawline, feeling the little muscles bunch and flex as her mouth traced the arrogant length, and then she nibbled with delicate fervour on the soft lobe of his ear.

He groaned, and in a muffled voice said, 'I think you'd better stop that, Kathy.'

Drunk with courage and delight, she whispered into his ear, 'Why? I like doing it. Don't you want me to?'

'Too much, you little sensualist,' he muttered. His hand came up and turned her head, forcing it into the lean brown column of his throat.

But she found things to relish there, too: the scent of him, masculine and subtle yet fiercely potent, the strength of his shoulders and the smooth swell of muscles beneath the cotton shirt.

Desire throbbed through her in a sensual beat, mindless, compulsive. She thought of the fact that this was the first time she had taken these privileges, the first time she had wanted to explore the intrinsic differences of a man's body.

Unashamed, her eyes slumbrous, she traced the sinews down his arm, kissed the blue veins of his wrist, watched his fingers curl as her tongue delicately tasted his palm, explored between his fingers.

In spite of the fact that he had to spend most of his time indoors his hands were not soft. They were not as callused as those of her father and other farmers she had known but they revealed signs of hard physical labour, as did the taut muscles and lithe form.

'How do you keep so fit?' she murmured in a dazzled smoky little voice.

'I swim. And I ride.'

'Ah, that explains these,' she said, her slender finger lingering on the hard pads above his palm.

'Mm hmm.' His hand slid up her arm to her shoulder, leaving a trail of fire behind it. Even as she wondered if her touch had done the same to him she surrendered to his.

'How about you?' he asked softly. 'You're soft, but sleek and strong with it.'

She leaned into him, biting gently at the bulge of muscle on his shoulder. 'Libby and I walk, Fiona and I exercise. And I mow lawns.'

'Lawns?'

'Hmm. When I'm not at university or swotting or producing essays I work for a man who has a lawn-mowing business.'

The words floated dreamily from her lips. Dazed by the sun and the day, the pleasant tiredness after swimming, the good food and the two glasses of wine she had had with it, she felt as though she were floating on a sea of sensation, lazily replete, unbearably stimulated.

A phrase from somewhere popped into her mind. '"Wine-dark sea",' she said in a slurred little voice.

'Are you slightly drunk?' he asked, his breath tickling her throat as he laughed.

'I don't think so. Although, I'm no great drinker, two glasses a night is my limit, so perhaps I am. If that's what it is, I rather like it.' She was talking nonsense, and she knew it. Drunk she might be, but it was not on the wine.

He smiled, his eyes gleaming with amusement as he lay back on the shady rug and pulled her with him. 'Sleep for a little while,' he said softly.

She wanted to object that she wasn't tired but her lashes weighed heavily down in spite of herself, and even as she snuggled into his shoulder she was asleep.

And woke to a feeling of rightness, of supreme pleasure and comfort. Her position was certainly not normal, and neither was the noise she could hear—a steady, rhythmic thudding that puzzled her until she worked out what it was. Even then, as the knowledge that it was someone's heartbeat percolated her brain, she still didn't know where she was.

But slowly, drowsily, she recalled that the soft hushing noise she heard was the sound of waves, and when a seagull mewed she realised that she was lying in André Hunter's arms on the beach at Motuiti, the little island.

She realised something else, too. Scarlet with mortification, she remembered that she had practically eaten him before he had finally decided she was drunk.

Humiliation of a particularly unbearable sort washed over her. Lying with her cheek on his shoulder, her body lightly, loosely pressed up against the warm, hard length of his, she felt as though she was never going to be able to look him in the eye again. What on earth must he think of her?

Beyond the steady rise and fall of his chest as he breathed, he didn't move. Slowly, cautiously, she opened her eyes and moved her head a little so that she could see his face. He too was asleep, those long lashes resting on the smooth skin, his mouth relaxed. Like that he didn't look so much like an eagle, she thought, striving to ignore the pangs of shame that clawed through her like barbed whips. Indeed, in repose his mouth was tender, as though the uncompromising authority that was so much a part of him was partly imposed by his will.

Although he didn't immediately open his eyes, she knew when he woke. The hint of vulnerability fled; it was like watching him don a mask, the way the inflexible toughness returned to his expression.

Then his heavy eyelids lifted, and he transfixed her with a cool green stare, limpid, cold as water in the polar seas. Her worst fears were immediately realised. Of course he despised her for her totally unforgivable behaviour. It had to have been the wine, she thought despairingly, but how to tell him that?

Suddenly his gaze warmed with amusement. 'Stop looking so guilty and horrified,' he drawled.

'I don't——' Colour rocketed through her skin. She swallowed and began again. 'I'm not normally so forward.'

'Pity,' he teased, lifting his head to kiss her lightly on the nose. 'There's no need for all that blushing and despairing, silly woman. I'd like to think that your charming, playful ardour was because you couldn't resist me, but I know perfectly well that two glasses of wine were too much for you.'

She bit her lip, then met his eyes with a candid, rather shamefaced smile. 'I can assure you,' she said a little flirtatiously, 'I don't get amorous every time I drink two glasses of wine!'

And held her breath, because it seemed that she had just gambled. And that the stakes were higher than anything else she had ever bet on: her ability to keep herself at university; her decision to come to Auckland and take a degree; even her fight to live her own life and not the one her parents had mapped out for her.

Laughing softly, he rolled over, holding her under him for a long, pulsating second so that her shy body felt the full imprint of his, the virile, seeking hardness and the weight. He looked into her face, his own shuttered, while leaping lights of fire illuminated the green of his eyes.

'Good,' he said with satisfaction as he left her and got to his feet, holding out his hand in a summons she obeyed with surprising meekness. As he pulled her up he said, 'Only with me, is it? Soon, I hope, you won't need wine to relax your inhibitions. Now, let's wake ourselves up with another swim, and we'll do a little exploring.'

That day marked the beginning of a magical time for her. While the year wound down to its close and New Zealand prepared for Christmas and the summer holidays, Kathy floated like a princess in a fairy-tale through the hot, humid days and nights, slowly coming more and more under André's spell.

He took her to dinner in restaurants she had only read of, choosing quiet secluded tables where they could talk without interruption. Occasionally people came over to greet him, but in the pleasantest manner André made it obvious that he didn't want to speak to anyone else. Most took his point and left immediately, but an occasional few were more persistent. Then she saw another André, a cold, incisive man whose razor-sharp tongue froze out even the most thick-skinned interloper.

They went to the theatre, and out to the wild west coast beaches—the masculine coast as the Maori people had called it—contrasting it with the sheltered serene beauty of the east coast and the gulf. Here she discovered yet another André Hunter, a man who enjoyed tramping through wild country.

'I find it helps me keep in touch with my soul,' he said simply.

And all the time they talked, she perhaps more than he, but he told her of his life growing up on the tropical island of New Caledonia with a mother and stepfather who didn't like him, until his high-school years when he came to live with his father and his stepmother in Gisborne. It was there that he had decided to follow his father into business. He didn't say, but it was clear that he had outgrown his father's essentially provincial base, and that his move to New Zealand's largest city was the logical one to make.

'No siblings?' she asked.

He shrugged, staring at the tempestuous wave pattern on the black beach below. 'No, no siblings. Like you, I'm alone. A stepsister, that's all. My stepmother's daughter from her first marriage; we grew away from each other when I left home.'

She nodded, feeling yet another sense of affinity with him.

But they had, she thought one night as she brushed her hair at the window and watched the street lights blossom, so much in common.

And one of the things was the violent attraction that flared between them. She touched her fingers to her throbbing mouth. Only a few minutes ago he had kissed her with something like desperation, but as on every occasion that was all that he had done. Each time he left her aching with frustration so that she spent much of the night tossing and turning in her bed.

She respected him for his respect for her, but she didn't need to be very experienced to know that he wanted her, and that he was holding back because he thought she was innocent, even naïve.

Her hand crept to clench between her breasts.

It was wonderful to feel so safe, so cherished, but in spite of everything each time they said goodnight she ached more and more for him to give in to the wildness of the passion they both felt.

CHAPTER THREE

WHEN Brent dropped her off at home after work the next day Kathy was hot, tired, and grubby, with grass-clippings clinging to her legs and her nose slightly sun-burned after a day spent mowing. Brent's ruggedly pleasant face was flushed too, in spite of the wide straw hat he habitually wore.

'Well, that's the week finished,' he said cheerfully. 'Going out tonight?'

He knew about André, and in spite of Libby's state-ments had shown no signs of being upset. So much for Libby.

'No, André has a business dinner—men only.' She pulled a face.

'I thought those went out with the Victorians. Would you like to come to the pictures with me? The Lido is showing that Japanese film you wanted to see so much.'

Smiling, she shook her head. 'No, thanks, that's sweet of you, but I think I'll get to bed early.'

'OK,' he said amiably, turning into the driveway. 'See you on Monday.'

As she got out she remembered something. Poking her head back into the van, she asked, 'Still nothing from the publishers?'

'No,' he sighed, pulling his mouth down at the corners in an exaggerated grimace of woe.

She frowned. 'How long is it since you sent it away?'

'Three months. I suppose it's too much to expect a large American publisher to be any faster. Unless they just parcelled it straight up and sent it back surface mail, of course.'

Kathy had read the science fiction novel that had kept Brent busy at nights and weekends over the past year, and was convinced it would sell. She said as much now and he grinned and leaned over to kiss her nose. 'I wish you were the editor looking at it,' he said in his teasing voice.

A low toot from behind made her pull away sharply. Her face lit up. 'Oh, it's André,' she said. 'Why don't you stay, Brent, and meet him?'

'No, I'd better get away, I've got a fair few things to do before it gets dark. See you, Katherine.'

She pulled a face at him; he always called her that because he said that Kathy was a child's name and she was a woman. Waving, she stood by the side of the bed of bearded irises while he went on around the circle and the sleek black bonnet of the Panthera stopped beside her.

With her radiant smile still lingering she bent to look in.

'Hop in,' André invited crisply.

She looked ruefully down at herself. 'No, I'll cover the seat in grass-clippings.'

'It can be cleaned.' She made to object again and he ordered, 'Get in, Kathy.'

'Oh,' she said as she slid in, 'I love it when you go all masterful and bossy.'

He smiled grimly, closed the door and ran his hand deliberately across her golden thigh. She felt her body clench, hidden muscles tightening in a sweet pain, an urgency that was driving her mad. Soon, she promised herself, her mouth curving in an unconsciously sensuous smile. Soon she would know how to appease that ache; she was in love with André, and she was certain that he loved her. Why else would he be so restrained, behaving with such rectitude that she was almost stifled with it?

'Was that the man you work for? Brent Whatsisname?'

'Brent Sheridan. Yes, that was him.'

The car moved a few feet and came to rest in the shade of the huge jacaranda tree. Brent gave a toot as the van took off back down the drive. Kathy thrust her arm out through the window and waved again.

'I didn't know that you were on kissing terms.' André was looking ahead through the windscreen, his lean hands still on the wheel, his voice remote, almost indifferent, but she picked up some strong emotion beneath the level tone.

Warily, she returned, 'We aren't.'

'He was kissing you when I came up behind you.'

'He kissed my nose, very casually.' If this was jealousy she wanted none of it. The man beside her sat as still as a predator marking out his prey, lean whipcord strength leashed until the perfect moment for the kill. She finished by saying sturdily, 'He's a friend, that's all. Like a big brother.'

Still in that even voice he said, 'Have you gone out with him?'

'I—yes, several times, in the middle of the year. But it wasn't——'

'Did he kiss you then?'

Anger coloured her tone. 'Yes. A chaste kiss goodnight at the end of the evening. I can assure you, André, that he is not interested in me as a woman.'

He turned his head, and she almost cried out at the crystalline dagger of his gaze. Uncannily echoing Libby, he said, 'He wouldn't have taken you out if he wasn't attracted.'

Head held so high that her neck ached, she retorted, 'André, you're being silly. There's nothing between us.'

Their gazes clashed, duelled, and held. Suddenly he relaxed, giving her a twisted smile. 'I didn't think I had it in me to be jealous,' he said ironically. 'I've always felt that it was the most degrading of emotions. Of course I believe you.'

Immensely relieved, she slid out of the car, dusting the strands of grass from the seat, using the little movement to hide her trembling reaction.

'Leave it,' he commanded deeply, coming around to her side.

She stood back and he bent and locked the door. It was cooler in the shade, but beads of sweat popped out across her top lip and at her fragile temples.

He kissed them away. 'You look worn out,' he murmured. 'Do you have to work so hard?'

His closeness made her languid. Smiling, she allowed herself to rest against him for a second before she moved away. 'It's a good job, really. It gets me out into the fresh air and I can fit in the hours with my lectures; it works very well. This is the busy period. The grass is growing like mad and everyone wants their place to look good for Christmas and the holidays.'

'What happens during the holiday season?'

She shrugged. 'Like every New Zealander, Brent goes to the beach for a fortnight, so the lawns just grow.'

'And you?'

'Oh, last summer holidays I worked for a friend of his who has the catering concession at the Zoo.'

He looked down at her as she unlocked the door into the house, his expression giving nothing away. 'How necessary is it for you to work during the holidays?'

'I can't afford not to,' she told him baldly.

'I see.' He was watching her face but as though he was not really seeing her, his brain working busily behind opaque eyes.

After a moment of this unnerving scrutiny she asked, 'Would you like to come in for a drink?'

'Sounds good. I'm dry.'

Her smile was a little tremulous. For the last week they had seen each other every day, and she was sure that like her he was becoming desperate. It was difficult to tell from his poker face, but she thought she was beginning to be able to read him now, to deduce what he was thinking from the tiny physical signs, the subtle body language that could be so much more truthful than words. She could sense the compelling need in him, the urgent male demands only kept in check by a ferocious will-power.

Up in the flat she poured them both a long glass of orange juice and opened the french windows on to the balcony to let some air into the stuffy room.

'Let's drink out here.' She had kicked off the sturdy boots she wore while she was mowing and was padding about in her bare feet. 'It's much cooler. Heavens, but it's been hot, hasn't it?'

As André relaxed in the long lounger that was Fiona's pride and joy he said idly, 'I'd have thought that if you wanted to save money you'd find less expensive lodgings. This must make a large hole in your budget.'

'It does, but Chris took a long lease on it. With Fiona and Libby's share I can just manage it.'

'I see. So your cousin left you to caretake.'

She smiled a little self-consciously, 'I suppose you could say so.'

Silence, sparked as all their silences were with the thrumming undercurrents that neither of them were yet prepared to acknowledge. The noise of traffic was a distant buzz, scarcely louder than the fat bumble-bee in the bougainvillaea flowers. Down below on the drive a mynah titupped across the gravel, its masked face turning from side to side. Kathy hated the greedy little robbers; she leaned over the rail and flung her arms wide. The bird took off with an indignant squawk and landed in the jacaranda tree from where it watched them spitefully.

'Childish,' André drawled lazily. 'Tell me about this cousin of yours.'

Always before she had noticed a faint hint of reservation in him when she talked of her cousin, so she had kept away from the subject. But now she said eagerly,

'Chris is an absolute darling. He knew how frustrated I was at home and encouraged me to break away, even offering to let me live with him. I think it was probably the only thing that stopped my parents having me declared a ward of court. They know him, of course; Uncle Phil and Aunt Laura live right next door. They knew I'd be safe with him.'

'Another big brother? Like Whatsisname?' he murmured, eyes almost closed as the westering sun dipped into the branches of the jacaranda.

'Brent? Chris is inclined to be too much so.' She laughed. 'He vetted everyone I went out with, fussed if I came home late from university, and made me eat decent meals. He also kept my parents off my back.'

'He sounds the perfect flatmate.' His eyes were narrowed to thin green slits, the long lashes casting shadows on his copper skin. 'Did he object to your going out with Brent?'

Kathy's heart lurched. Sprawled in the lounger, he looked like a great lithe cat, all smooth lines and sleek power beneath the exquisitely cut business clothes he was wearing. He had taken off his jacket and the fine pin-striped shirt clung to his arms and torso, while the tailored trousers hinted at the strong muscled thighs beneath.

'Yes,' she said thinly, scarcely knowing what she said. 'Oh, he liked him, but he thought he was too old.'

'How old is he?'

'Nearly thirty, I think.'

'Not *too* old,' he said, his voice remote.

A hot tide surged through her body, settling heavily, inevitably in the fork. Her breasts tightened; without looking down she moved a little so that the peaking buds would not be so obvious beneath her T-shirt. Oh, God, she thought, made faint by an overpowering need, I wish I didn't have to think! I wish I could just surrender to this incredible hunger.

Aloud, in a voice she tried hard to make even, she said, 'You look hot. And tired.'

'Mmm.' He sat his glass down and stretched, muscles rippling and popping beneath the fine cotton. 'I'll be glad to get to the bach,' he murmured.

With a suddenly dry mouth she looked away and concentrated on what she knew of his bach. It was his hideaway, the small cabin in the woods that everyone needed for the refreshment of their soul. Only his was not on the beach where most baches were. André retreated to the hills of the far north, with bush and peace and quiet all around.

Flatly, the words coming with leaden precision, she asked, 'When do you go?'

'Boxing Day.' He opened his eyes and caught her looking at him with her heart in her eyes. 'Why don't you come with me?' he asked calmly.

Her response was automatic. 'I—I couldn't,' she said.

Holding her prisoner with that knowing gaze, he said, 'Yes, you can. All that's holding you back is worry about what your parents would say. I thought you left them so that you could lead your own life.'

She looked down at the hands clasped so tightly together in her lap. She knew what her agreement to go with him would mean. They would become lovers.

Her heart gave one gigantic throb, and then settled down as her thoughts raced wildly through her brain. It seemed so—cold-blooded, so unromantic, so—*planned*.

This thought was followed by another, shaming her. She was, she thought scornfully, just like a child, thinking that spontaneous sex was more romantic, more passionate. Perhaps she wanted to duck responsibility by being seduced into making love, instead of making a decision to do it.

But, oh, it was a step off the edge and into the unknown. Her doubtful eyes traced the bold, uncompromising contours of his face as she wondered if this was some sort of test. He had never told her that he loved her; he had not mentioned plans for any future together.

Painfully, she said, 'I don't know, André. I'll have to think about it. For one thing, I need some money to live on next year. If I don't work these holidays I won't be able to go back to university.'

'I can make sure you don't lose by it,' he said indolently.

Humiliated colour scorched apricot across her cheeks. 'I didn't mean that,' she said with stiff pride, getting to her feet.

He laughed softly and caught her hand, pulling her down on top of him. 'Don't be so prickly. I wouldn't be paying you for anything you cared to give me, merely making sure you didn't lose by keeping me company.'

'That's splitting hairs,' she muttered. 'André, let me up. I'm all sweaty, and I'll cover your beautiful suit in grass——'

'How you do go on about that grass,' he complained, nuzzling into her throat. 'I like you covered in grass clippings, it gives you a fresh, earthy appeal. Mmm, you smell like warm woman, sweet and tropical and luscious, and you taste of salt and musk—erotic as hell.' His tongue touched the little pulse in her throat, and as his hands smoothed over the firm mounds of her buttocks and on down the sleek length of her thigh her heart threatened to burst through her breast.

'Oh, I can't,' she whispered frantically, although her treacherous body refused to pull away.

'Yes, you can.' But he lifted his head, and looked deliberately into her face, his eyes gleaming with satisfaction. 'However, I'm not going to persuade you this way. You'll make up your mind without any physical pressure from me, otherwise I'll never be able to convince either of us that I didn't over-persuade you.'

How she wished he would! It would make things so much easier to be rendered mindless with need, the decision made for her when she was clamorous with desire.

Angry with him because he was being so reasonable when she wanted him to be as much a prey of emotions as she was, she sighed, fighting to force her mind into a logical frame. His responsible attitude was a measure of his regard for her; infuriating though it was, she was glad that he respected her.

So she smiled mistily into his face and kissed his mouth, dragging her lips away before they had a chance to cling. 'You are so good to me,' she said softly.

Something moved in his face, a swift flicker of some nameless emotion. She thought she felt him stiffen, but a moment later he was dumping her on to the floor, saying as he got up, 'The decision has to be yours, Kathy. In the meantime I have to go—this wretched dinner could be important, and I don't want to be late.'

She let him out, and waved a little wistfully from the balcony, then spent ages wandering fruitlessly about, trying to make up her mind whether to go with him to his bach or not.

'I see,' Libby observed later, after watching Kathy prowl around the room for the third time, 'by your lean and hungry look, that he hasn't got you into bed yet.'

Kathy flushed, cursing her lack of sophistication. 'André is not like most other men,' she said in reply.

'Yes. I find that surprising. Most men would take one look at you, ripe for the picking and as pretty as a picture, and whip you into bed so fast you wouldn't know how you got there.'

'André has a little more subtlety than that,' Kathy said with pride.

Another silence, one in which she could feel Libby's eyes on her, then the other woman said with a tentativeness that was unusual for her, 'Kathy, are you still a virgin?'

'I——' Her wild flush was answer enough.

Libby said on a sigh, 'So you are—I thought you probably were. Look, I don't want you hurt, love. But have you——?'

She was interrupted by the imperative summons of the telephone. Kathy snatched up the receiver, thankful for the reprieve from what she judged was likely to be Libby at her most maternal. It was Brent, his voice so excited that she had to beg him to slow down before she could understand.

'The book,' he shouted. 'Dear heart, the letter was waiting for me and they want it! They think it's good, and it's going to be their leading title!'

'Oh, *Brent*! That's wonderful! I'm so happy for you!'

'Happy enough to celebrate with me? I thought I'd go out to dinner and drink champagne in the best restaurant I can afford. How does that sound?'

She hesitated, before asking diffidently, 'But haven't you—isn't there someone else you'd rather celebrate with?'

'I've rung the family,' he told her, his voice still ringing with excitement, 'and no, there's no one else. I'd like you to come, love; you deserve to—after all, you encouraged me to keep going when I'd decided to give up.'

'You wouldn't have given up,' she said. 'You couldn't have given up, and yes, of course I'll help you celebrate.'

Putting the telephone down, she turned rather defensively to Libby, who was watching with an elaborately expressionless face. She explained, finishing with a defiance that irritated her. 'He had no one else to go with him.'

'No one else he *wants* to go with him,' Libby corrected. 'What's André going to think?'

'He'll understand.' But she recalled his jealousy that afternoon with an odd sinking sensation in the pit of her stomach.

Something of her thoughts must have appeared in her face because Libby persisted shrewdly, 'He doesn't look like the sort of man who is prepared to share.'

Kathy's mouth firmed. 'It won't be sharing! If he's that unreasonable he'll just have to suffer for it. Brent has been fantastic to me, and there's no one I'd rather see have such good luck.'

'OK, OK,' Libby said, backing off, her hands held in front of her. 'You know the man. And I think you're quite right, of course, only André Hunter strikes me as being definitely possessive.'

Unfortunately Kathy knew how possessive he was, but she also knew that she couldn't leave Brent alone on this happiest of nights for him. So she wore her very best outfit, a slender skirt and blouse she had made in a rich satin-look acetate and rayon material that had cost her the earth even in a remnant sale.

However, she thought as she applied lipstick, it was worth it. The high throat-covering neckline emphasised her cleft chin, and the clear paprika colour suited her to perfection.

'Well!' Libby said. 'I love that outfit. Only you could wear that colour and get away with it.'

'Thanks.' Uneasily she looked out of the window. 'If André rings——' she began before she could stop herself.

'Yes?'

She flushed. 'Oh, it doesn't matter, he won't ring.'

Libby cocked an eyebrow but mercifully left it at that.

Brent was delighted to see her, his expression so elated that he was almost handsome. Deciding that she was not going to let her concern about André's reaction spoil his evening for him, Kathy met and matched his exuberance, trying very hard to celebrate as enthusiastically as he did.

It should have been a wonderful evening; at least Brent enjoyed himself immensely. And although her brain was teased by memories of that first evening with André,

Kathy didn't allow it to show because Brent's delight in her company was transparent and strangely warming. He teased her, making her laugh with his wild fantasies of his future life as a writer, clearly doing his best to entertain her. She thought of André, whose eyes could darken with a fierce passion that sent shudders of sensation through her, yet, for all the heat and the desire, remained somehow withdrawn.

Brent's expression disclosed no such ardour, yet she felt a much greater closeness to him. Sternly repressing such disloyal thoughts, she smiled and replied to her companion's sallies with an easy response that seemed to her confused mind yet another sort of disloyalty.

All in all she was glad when at last, much later than she had expected because he insisted on going on to a nightclub, they were once more in front of the house.

'Who'd have thought,' she mused as he switched off the engine, 'when we were here this afternoon, that we'd be here again tonight? I'm so thrilled for you, Brent.'

He grinned and jumped down from the van, striding around to help her out. 'So, by God, am I,' he said largely as he lifted her down to the ground. She staggered a little, and he grabbed her. 'Careful, dear heart, we don't want to ladder those stockings, do we?'

She was laughing, laughed again as he cracked a joke, and then the laughter fled, to be replaced by sheer cold terror as André's voice came smoothly out of the darkness.

'Get your hands off her,' he said.

Both whirled in his direction, Kathy's eyes widening endlessly when she saw the silhouette of the Panthera parked in the deep shade of the tree. But André was a darker shadow. He had come upon them as silently as a figure of the night, a wraith, a hunter intent on death.

'It's all right,' Kathy said, instinctively protecting Brent. 'He was only helping me out.'

'I saw what he was doing.' André's voice cut into Brent's, effortlessly overriding it. 'Listen to me,' he said thinly, 'and don't make me say this again. Kathy is not for you. Get the hell out of here and don't try to see her again.'

'I don't take orders from anyone.' Brent's normally pleasant voice was crisp and curt. 'If Katherine wants me to leave her I will.'

'Kathy?'

Only one word, but the tone was as implacable as that of a judge handing down a death sentence. An icy chill swept over her. She said just as quietly, 'Brent has just had a book accepted by an American publisher, André. His very first book.'

'I am very happy for him.' Sarcasm sharpened the words, then transmuted his next into a flat threat. 'Next time, Sheridan, find someone else to celebrate with. Come on, Kathy, time to go in.'

Brent said, 'Katherine?'

She drew a deep breath, furious with André for making her choose, and despairing because she thought there must be some way of tackling the situation that wouldn't leave them all with a nasty taste in their mouths. But if there was, she didn't know it.

At last, when the silence had grown so thick she thought she could see it, she said sadly, 'Goodbye, Brent.'

He turned and got back into the van and drove off down the drive. They stood perfectly still until the sound of his engine had died away, and then she demanded heatedly, 'How could you?'

'If I weren't so sure that for you it was perfectly innocent,' he said still in that same flat icy voice, 'I'd have knocked him to the ground.'

'He was so thrilled,' she said hotly. 'And now you've spoilt it.'

He hauled her into his arms. 'And you're so bloody naïve,' he snarled. 'Couldn't you see that part of the reason for his excitement was because you were with him? He's in love with you, but you belong to me, you're mine.'

His mouth was cruel, a punishment that ravaged hers until he groaned and lifted his head. 'I'm sorry,' he muttered. 'I've been sitting here waiting for you, working myself up into a stupid jealous rage, and when I saw him catch you in his arms I wanted to kill him.'

'You don't need to be jealous,' she whispered, her heart in her voice. 'I went with him because he said there was no one else to celebrate with him, but don't you know I love you, André? I'd die sooner than let anyone else make love to me.'

He was very still, and then he pulled her back into the Panthera, stretching out across the back seat, his mouth hot and seeking as he kissed her. 'You fascinating, enchanting little witch,' he whispered. 'You've got me so tied up in knots I can't think straight.'

His hand slid up her bare back beneath the blouse. She felt the fingers fumble slightly with the catch of her bra but almost immediately he unclipped the clasp. He's too good at this, she thought, but the cynical little observation was gone in a wave of sensual pleasure as his hand smoothed over the silken skin of her back and moved around to cup her small breast, the thumb passing so lightly over the peaking nipple that it felt like a feather, incredibly, erotically, abrasive against the thrusting flesh.

He had done this before, touched her with exquisite tenderness, but this time he pushed the satin right up and for the first time in her life she felt a man's mouth on her breasts. It galvanised her into a wild ecstasy; she gasped, and clenched her hands against his chest, shudders sizzling through her as he tasted the small peaks, before his mouth closed hotly, almost savagely around one and he suckled her.

It was like being entranced, held in a sorcery of dark magic where the only reality was his mouth and his hands and the long, strong length of him taut and hard against her in the car, his scent like incense on the drugged air, her body held in chains of sensual servitude, straining towards some unknowable, unreachable pinnacle of sensation.

She was caught by fever, wanting to clench her muscles tightly, yet strangely languid, ready to flow around him like liquid honey tinged with fire. Sharp little shocks ran from her breasts through her body, changing her, altering the Kathy Townsend who had never known this rapture to a new and different woman. She whimpered and he lifted his mouth from her aching breast.

'What is it?' he asked, his breath playing sensuously over the damp skin.

She gasped, 'I don't know.'

He laughed, and said softly, 'I do.'

He touched the other hard little peak, licked it as delicately as a cat until it stood forth proud and demanding, and then it too was enveloped in his voracious mouth. Sighing, because that was what she had wanted, she slid her hand beneath his shirt, stroking slowly along the swell and curve of muscle, revelling in the satin texture of his skin beneath the fine swirls of hair. Her hand touched his masculine nipple and she played softly with it, enjoying the sudden tension in him, realising with passionate surprise that he liked it too, this sensuous caressing.

Slowly, as he made himself master of her responses, she explored, her fingertips so sensitive she thought fancifully that she must have lost a surplus layer of skin.

And then she began to shake, a crescendo of sensation building. She knew what she wanted, knew too that it was impossible, and in her longing she pressed herself against him, her small slight body tense and aching with desire, the age-old hunger to yield in a surrender that was paradoxically a victory.

His arms wrapped around her; for long seconds she felt every muscle and bone, every long sinew, the beat of his heart and the breaths he took, moulded against her, and she reached around his broad shoulders and offered herself to him like a flower to the sun.

'Not here,' he groaned, kissing her mouth, the cleft in her chin, her ear. 'I haven't made love in a car since I was a randy teenager, for heaven's sake.'

He buried his burning face in her throat, then sat up and put her away. The soft glow of her blouse gleamed in the dim light; he moved it aside, and looked at her breasts. 'Like satin,' he said deeply. 'Clover-tipped, and as sweet as clover flowers.' His mouth lingered on each proud aureole and then he pulled the blouse straight and sat her up, his deft hands reclipping her bra.

'You'd better get yourself into some sort of order,' he observed, 'in case your mother hen is still up.'

Insensibly chilled by his matter-of-fact attitude, she climbed out of the car and shimmied her skirt straight, watching with eyes that burned as he buttoned up the shirt she had somehow unfastened, and tucked it into his trousers with the swift movements of familiarity.

But as she turned to go inside he said quietly, 'I'm not going to be able to hold out much longer, Kathy. You have to make a decision soon.'

She thought she stood before a closed door. On the other side was—what? Delight? Despair? The transports of paradise or the agonies of purgatory?

She had no idea, although some instinctual part of her warned that although the door was still closed she had already gone too far to back away.

But at the moment she wondered why her greatest impulse was to smooth away the narrow deep line between his brows and offer him some sort of surcease from the frustration she sensed in him, the same frustration that tore through her.

'Yes,' she said, rendered almost silent by the flood of pure emotion through her. 'I'll go north with you.'

He stood very still, his eyes locked on to hers. Her breath caught in her throat but she met that burning, searing gaze, a shy little smile curling around her mouth.

Quietly he asked, 'And will you share my bed, little witch? Because there is only one there.'

She nodded, aware of the enormity of her decision, yet determined not to go back on it now.

'I want to hear you say it,' he said softly.

She swallowed nervously but said, 'I'll sleep with you, André.'

An odd little smile touched his lips; perhaps it was the shifting light of the moon through the feathery leaves of the jacaranda, but to her it seemed humourless, almost cruelly anticipatory. Then it was gone and he was kissing her forehead, disappointing her because she wanted him to take another of those deep, drugging kisses that stopped the still small voice of her conscience.

He took her up the stairs and kissed her again outside the door with heart-shaking tenderness, so that she stumbled through the door, lost in the world of magic he had woven about her.

'Are you all right?'

She jumped at Libby's anxious voice, stared to see her rise from the sofa, yawning, still dressed in jeans and a thin cotton sweatshirt that showed off her magnificent figure.

'What?' Dazed, she wandered over towards the older woman, her eyes shining like stars in deep waters.

'Yes, I can see that you are,' Libby muttered, with an ironic smile. 'When he turned up on the doorstep I had to tell him where you were.' She gave a small shiver, unfaked. 'Not a man you can lie to easily, I discovered. I thought I'd better wait up to apologise.'

She looked tired, as though she had slept, but uncomfortably. 'It's all right,' Kathy said gently. 'He was angry but——'

'He looked angry enough to kill.'

Kathy smiled. 'No, André is too much in control to behave like an idiot. I explained what happened and he was a bit curt but it was all quite polite.'

Libby looked curiously at her. 'I see,' she said again. 'Ah, well, that'll teach me to over-react.'

'Thank you,' Kathy said, smiling, her dimple playing elusively, her expression warmly affectionate.

Libby closed her eyes, then shrugged. 'Never mind,' she said, almost as though speaking to herself. 'See you in the morning.'

Kathy woke late, with the sun making pleasing patterns on the curtains, and lay still in her narrow bed, wondering why her mind should be so clear and definite. She knew that she was going to spend the holidays with André, she knew that when he wanted to make love to her she would give him everything she could, spend her capital of love with no thought of interest.

He hadn't said that he loved her; she thought he did, but it didn't really matter, she decided dreamily, stretching with a languorous satisfaction beneath the blanket. Her love was enough for both of them. Whatever he felt for her had to be more than sheer lust, or he would never have waited so long for her to make up her mind, especially not when a man of his experience must have sensed that with a little pressure he could have had her surrender weeks ago. She would go with him, and she would love him, and he would learn to love her.

And I had better go to the doctor, she thought.

Her mouth straightened from its tremulous curve; for a moment she looked as though she might be about to weep. But then she made an effort, springing out of bed, her slender body golden in the fresh light as she ran across to the window and hurled the curtains back to greet the sweet-smelling day.

Someone pounded on her door. 'Phone,' Fiona said in her husky early morning voice.

It was Brent, his voice anxious as he asked what had happened.

'Nothing,' she said, flushing a little at his snort of disbelief. 'No, honestly, nothing did, Brent. André is not unbalanced.'

'He didn't sound particularly balanced last night! If ever a man was holding himself on a short leash, he was. Are you sure you're OK?'

'Of course I am.' She gave a bewildered little smile. 'Honestly, what with you and Libby—André is not a monster, he's in full control of his temper. He was angry, but wouldn't you have been furious if you saw your girl-friend apparently kissing another man?'

'Yes, but——'

'Brent, he's not into beating, or violence of any sort. He understood when I told him what had happened.'

'Well, if you say so.'

She shrugged, her voice firming. 'I do say so.'

'All right, then, dear heart.'

'Have you come down to earth yet?'

'What? Oh, you mean the book? Yes, with a thump.' She said firmly, 'You must get on with the next one, because it's going to be even better.'

He laughed. 'I hope. Well, if you're sure you're OK...'

'Of course I am. But thank you for ringing.'

When she had hung up she wandered dreamily into the kitchen, hugging herself, a small reminiscent smile playing around her soft mouth.

'Look at her,' Libby grumbled. 'High drama and wild sex the night before and she comes out looking like a rose the next morning. Hell, I wish I were eighteen again!'

'No high drama,' Kathy corrected firmly, adding with a deeper blush, 'and no sex, either.'

Libby lifted a sceptical eyebrow. 'OK, so you're still virgo, but from the look of you as you wandered in last night it's barely intacta!'

'You're embarrassing the girl.' Fiona looked from beneath her lashes across at the older woman. 'You know, anyone would think that lurking beneath your motherly interest in Kathy is a far from maternal interest in the gorgeous André.'

'Don't be an idiot!' Libby's sharp response took them by surprise, herself included. After a moment she relaxed and said with a derisory smile, 'He's younger than me, for heaven's sake.'

'So he is,' Fiona murmured, and changed the subject by asking if anyone had picked up the paper yet.

Kathy sat looking out of the window, a small smile playing about her mouth. She was wondering what sort of clothes one took to a romantic tryst in Northland.

CHAPTER FOUR

'But, Kathy, I thought you were going home for Christmas!'

'No, I'm staying here,' she said calmly. 'I can't afford the fares home.'

Libby frowned. 'Well, then, who are you going to spend Christmas Day with? Or don't I need to ask?'

'No one. André is going down to be with his father and stepmother at Gisborne.'

'But—you'll be alone! You can't spend Christmas alone, love.'

Pushing a damp copper tendril back from her brow, Kathy shrugged. 'Don't worry, Lib, I'll have a nice quiet day. I'm going to ring my parents.'

'It sounds awful,' Libby said slowly. 'Look, why don't you come home with me? We always have a big family Christmas and one more is not going to make any difference.'

Her family lived in Whangarei, a small city a couple of hours drive north of Auckland.

'That's very sweet of you,' Kathy said affectionately, 'but André is picking me up on Boxing Day, so I'll be all right.'

'Picking you up? What for? Auckland's dead for the fortnight after Christmas.'

Kathy coloured delicately. 'Yes, well, we won't be in Auckland. We're going up to his place at Whangaroa.'

'You're what?' Libby's voice was sharp with dismay, and something like anger. She stared at Kathy, her expression set as she made an obvious effort to control her emotions. 'Kathy, are you sure? I know he's stunning, and you're head over heels in love with him, but for God's sake think what you're doing! The man's light-years ahead of you in sophistication, and a hell of a lot tougher than you'll ever be.'

Kathy's mouth pulled into a stubborn line. 'I know that. But I do love him.'

'I know.' Libby sat down, all expression erased from her face. 'I remember,' she said after a moment with a wry smile. 'Oh, I remember very well what first love is like. All fire and desire. But he could hurt you very badly.'

Kathy shrugged. 'Yes, I know,' she said solemnly. Her face softened, became as radiant as her golden eyes. 'I don't think he will, though,' she finished with a heart-breakingly confident lilt in her voice.

Libby looked up at her and groaned, then gave a mocking, self-derisory smile. 'All right, how about coming home with me and asking him to pick you up from our place?' she said. 'I'm not going to be happy thinking of you down here on your own on Christmas Day.'

Kathy didn't much like the idea either. She had hoped that André would ask her to go with him to Gisborne, but when he had mentioned in passing that his stepmother was not well, still recovering from a death in the family, she had accepted that there was no place for her with him. Not yet, anyway. It was this thought, hugged close to her like a delicious secret, that helped her view a lonely Christmas with equanimity.

'Are you sure your mother won't mind?' she asked, wavering.

'I am certain. The more the merrier as far as she's concerned. Then you'll only be an hour or so from Whangaroa. Where exactly is his place there, anyway?'

'You turn off just north of Kaeo village and travel for about ten miles inland. He said it's on the right going in—just a track through the bush, apparently.'

'Sounds idyllic,' Libby said lazily. 'OK, so that's what we'll do.'

Kathy smiled. 'Thank you,' she said, the husky note in her voice more pronounced than usual.

Libby looked suddenly older. 'Don't thank me,' she said, shortly for her. 'No one should have to be alone at Christmas.'

Startling them both, Kathy gave her a sudden unexpected hug, then, somewhat embarrassed, whirled into her room to finish the skirt she was making.

Just back from chasing the results of her last paper, she was still elated at the excellent pass she had scored. That meant that she had done better than she'd expected on every paper. For a moment she thought of her parents, wishing that they could exult with her. Wistfully she wondered whether they had changed their minds. Then her face altered, became happy, even a little gleeful once more.

As her sewing-machine whirred she grinned, although she knew a momentary pang of guilt. She had used some of her savings to splash out on clothes, so next year she was going to have to economise severely. André had said nothing more about paying her during the holidays; just as well, as she had no intention of taking money from him.

But perhaps, she thought hopefully, her eyes becoming misty with dreams, perhaps she would be in a position to accept money from him without losing independence. Perhaps by then they would be engaged.

Libby's doubts had tarnished her happiness a little, but she banished them with determination. Libby had suspected André right from the start, but Libby was a born cynic.

And, after all, at the very beginning Kathy herself had wondered what he saw in her very ordinary person. Now she no longer worried. He had made no attempt to seduce her, he had given her the opportunity to back out if she wanted to, he hadn't used the blazing attraction between them to coerce or persuade her into doing anything.

He had been 'a verray, parfit gentil knyght' she thought dreamily, quoting from the *Canterbury Tales*.

And in a week's time she would be with him in his bach. Alone. With three whole weeks ahead of them, long, lazy, summer days spent with the only man she would ever love. Her skin heated as she felt the familiar shock of desire. She was so thankful that she had not made love with any of the boys who had importuned her at school. Not that she had had much opportunity— her parents had made sure of that. But she was glad that André was going to be the first and the last. She only hoped that her inexperience wouldn't put him off. Still, she thought with a secret inner thrill, he knew that she hadn't made love, that he would be the first. She hadn't tried to hide how green she was.

Christmas at Libby's home was noisy and cheerful and very casual, and although she missed André keenly Kathy enjoyed herself. But she couldn't restrain her excitement and the anticipation that fired her blood when he arrived after lunch on Boxing Day, instantly reducing Libby's irreverent family to a respectful attention. The men and boys drooled over the Panthera, the women over its driver.

Although he was affable and friendly, his blazing vitality seemed a little dimmed, Kathy thought, gazing at his beloved face with anxiety. But of course he would be tired, he had already driven all the way from Gisborne, at least five hours' travel in the heat and the holiday madness on the roads.

'Take care of her,' Libby said as she waved goodbye.

He looked down at her, something in his expression catching Kathy's attention, a kind of speculative arrogance she had not seen there before. And Libby's expression was definitely challenging as she stood there in her shorts and a thin shirt that showed off her magnificent breasts.

'Of course,' he said with an offhand indifference that drove the colour from Libby's skin.

She met his eyes squarely for a long significant moment, then shrugged, saying lightly, 'I'll see you after the holidays, then. Have fun, Kathy.'

'I will.' When they had gone a few miles she said apologetically, 'Libby's a bit inclined to fuss.'

'Is that what it was?'

'What do you mean?'

His mouth twisted in a rather unpleasant smile. 'It's all right; Libby and I understand each other very well.'

Wondering what he meant by that, Kathy forced herself to relax. The nervousness that crawled through her was normal, compounded as it was by excitement and a singing awareness of his closeness.

To keep the wild cocktail of emotions under control she stared out of the window, asking questions about the sunburnt countryside of Northland, listening to his answers and his observations as he pointed out places of interest along the way. Once she asked him how his stepmother was, and he said curtly that she was still not very well.

Clearly he didn't want to talk about it, so she relapsed into silence, looking out of the window with dream-shadowed eyes all the way to Kaeo, a sleepy little village with some quaint old buildings beside a tidal river. A few miles further on he turned off the highway. The sun beat down and the dust rose behind them as they snaked alongside a small river, mangrove-bound for some miles before changing its character to a gravel-bottomed creek amid kowhai and cabbage trees.

The traffic had been heavy all the way with Aucklanders fleeing the city for the summer delights of beach and bush, and André had had to concentrate on the road. He was, as she already knew, an excellent driver, but it wasn't until they were on the narrow gravel road that she realised just how good he was, his lean hands steadily controlling the wheel as the big car dealt with ruts and pot-holes and corrugations.

After a few miles the road began to climb through second-growth bush, cool and tall, with cicadas buzzing. They must have been at least twenty minutes off the main highway when André nosed the car into a gate almost hidden in the trees. Kathy leaned forward to open her door but he shook his head.

'No, I'll do it, the gate hasn't been open for a while.'

She watched with adoring eyes as he heaved the gate open, muscles straining beneath the casual knit shirt he wore. The drive in was rutted, but the Panthera coped and after a few hundred metres they emerged from the trees into a small area of ungrazed grass. In front of them was a house, old although newly painted, but it was not that which stopped the breath in Kathy's lungs.

On two sides the house was surrounded by paddock that eased into bush-clad hills, but to the north and east the ground fell away, and spread out below was the most beautiful view in the world, a summer-hazed panorama of blue hills and trees, smooth, smiling farmland, and, beyond that and on out to the horizon, the great shining slab of the sea.

'Oh,' she whispered on a long exhalation of delight.

'You like it?'

'I love it! I thought the view from the top of the Brynderwyn hill was magnificent, but this is superb.'

He was looking straight ahead, his profile a hawkish slash against the golden landscape. 'Yes,' he said simply. 'Right, let's get the gear out.'

The bach was basic; a bedroom with a small bathroom, a living-room with the kitchen along one wall and glass doors on the other leading to a long veranda that ran along the northern side, so that the view was the focal point of the whole house.

Kathy despised herself for blushing when he carried her case into the bedroom and dumped it on to the unmade bed, but blushed again as he said casually, 'I'll let you put your clothes away. The left-hand wardrobe is mine.'

And she wondered jealously how many other women he had brought there.

It took her five minutes to unpack, but a considerably longer time to help him stow away the enormous amount of food he had brought. 'The nearest store is fifteen miles away,' he said casually in answer to her astonished exclamation, 'and I like to stay here once I get here.'

'No trips to the beach?'

He shrugged. 'There's a pool in the creek to swim in, and I can sunbathe anywhere, naked if I want to. Why would I want to go to the beach?'

'Why indeed?' she retorted, striving to match his worldliness, to hide the *frisson* of awareness his words gave her. She had never seen him—or any man—naked. Soon, she thought, thinking of the huge double bed she had just made up. A secret heat scorched through her.

She peered through her lashes at his angular face as he put the last of the provisions into the fridge. Why hadn't he kissed her, shown her some of the desire hidden below that enigmatic surface? Of course he wouldn't at Libby's place, in front of them all, and there had been no opportunity in the car. But surely now...? She even opened her mouth to ask him, then closed it again.

When the house was tidy and ready for occupancy he took her to see the pool, a romantic little oval above a waterfall that burbled down the steep hill separating them from the rest of the world. She looked around, admiring the pongas, the graceful treeferns that grew thickly around it, and the serene, still ambience of the bush. Dragon-flies skimmed gracefully across the surface of the water, and from somewhere she could hear the slow humming of bees.

'Beehives,' he said, and led her through white dog-daisies and cow-parsley and long, sweet-smelling grass to a small sleepy corner of the paddock, tucked in an angle of bush that sheltered it from the prevailing winds. Three beehives stood there, their inhabitants conducting their business with single-minded efficiency. 'I have a friend who likes manuka honey, and this is as good a place to gather it as any.'

She looked around, smiling at the airy plates of cow-parsley, seething with bees. 'I hope he likes cow-parsley honey too,' she said.

'I suppose he does. How would you like a swim?'

Insensibly chilled by his matter-of-fact behaviour, she said quietly, 'Yes, I'm hot and sticky.'

'What's the matter?' When she didn't answer his mouth twisted. 'Did you expect me to make love to you the minute we got here? The greed of youth, I suppose. Sorry—I prefer to savour these things.'

She looked at him gravely. 'You're only eight years older than I am.' It wasn't what she had wanted to say but she didn't know how to ask him if her mother was correct, if men no longer respected a woman when she had made love to them. Only they hadn't made love yet. Did the contempt begin with the surrender, the agreement? If this was so she thought her heart might break.

'Eight years.' He smiled, his lashes hiding his thoughts, his face a magnificent mask in the gilding sun. 'Not long, I'll agree, in time. But in experience, Kathy, I'm so much older than you that I might as well be in another generation.'

Was that it? Did he regret the fact that she was a virgin? Because she was inexperienced, or because he felt guilty at giving her that experience?

She slipped her hand into his, trying not to notice that his fingers closed around hers for only a brief second.

'I made the decision to come here,' she said softly. 'You didn't have to coax me or persuade me.'

'No. I thought I might have to.' He looked down into her earnest face, his own bland yet vaguely chilling. 'You were eager to come, weren't you?'

She nodded. 'Yes, I'm glad to be here.'

'Good, because I am too,' he said softly.

But the unease stayed with her. During the long hours of that afternoon his withdrawn attitude became more like an armour of impregnability. She found herself chattering—like a schoolgirl, she thought with disgust at her own ineptitude, and stumbled into silence at his sardonic glance.

Where was the rapport she had cherished? What was happening to them?

Fear began to build in her, a fear that she was unable to counter because it was too vague, based on nothing but a faint sense of betrayal, some inchoate suspicion that had been building since his arrival at Libby's home.

Yet in spite of that bewildering coolness he was perfectly pleasant; he just wasn't the same man who had made such passionate love to her, talked to her about everything, listened to her with such absorbed and absorbing interest. Jumpy, her nerves stretched unbearably, she told herself that it was only because tonight they were going to become lovers. Like her, he was tense. It was important to him.

She was still trying to convince herself of this when she lay on the lounger, lifting her face to the last warmth of the descending sun. Opening her eyes a slit, she allowed herself the fugitive luxury of watching him. He was reading, his face silhouetted by the golden radiance, the imperious arrogance of his features very pronounced. Like that, she thought, repressing a shiver, he looked—cruel, like some bold warrior of ancient times, barbarous and without mercy.

'Are you hungry?' he asked suddenly, looking up from his book.

She jumped, her eyes sliding away. 'I—yes.'

Anything was better than sitting next to him like this, so near that she could smell his faint, exciting masculine scent, so far that she might as well be on the other side of the moon.

'I'll get dinner,' he said, getting to his feet. 'You stay here and watch the night crawl over the countryside.'

She tried to do as he told her, obediently looking out to sea as the dusk came up from the east and spread like a mantle over the hills and valleys, the bold volcanic crags and the silver threads of streams. Lights twinkled in the farmhouses, small moving beams revealed where the main road led on to the north. Listening to the quiet sounds he made in the kitchen area, she thought she had never felt so alone in all her life.

And it was useless to tell herself that it was because of her mother's conditioning. If André had kissed her just once she would have thrown every precept her mother had tried to drum into her over the windmill.

Something was wrong, and she was going to have to find out what it was.

The cleft in her chin grew more pronounced as she lifted it high; with an urgent courage that held the seeds of panic she went into the small room, determined to have it out.

'Ah, you're hungry,' he said casually, after an unsmiling survey of her set face. 'It's ready. I thought cold meat and salad for tonight, as it's easy and we're both tired. We can organise something more elaborate tomorrow night if we feel like it. We'll have it out on the deck, I think. Set the table, will you?'

She took the knives and forks he held out to her and set them on the small table, then watched as he brought out a bowl of salad and a plate with sliced cold meat on it. He looked over her small, tense figure with inscrutable eyes.

'The bread's over there too,' he said. 'And some cheeses, if you'd like to bring them across.'

Frozen by his detached, impersonal attitude, she got them, washed her hands and sat down, stiff and silent as he politely asked her what she wanted. Her hand clenched. Instead of answering she asked desperately, 'André, what is the matter?'

He was breaking a roll, his lean fingers very dark against the white bread. She couldn't look at his face when she spoke, but as his fingers stilled she dredged up her courage and saw that inscrutable mask shatter into something much more dreadful, a harsh ruthlessness that made her shrink away from him.

'Would you say you were truthful?' he asked obliquely.

She stared at him in total bewilderment. 'What do you mean?'

'Just that. Does the thought of telling a lie fill you with horror, or would you lie if it was expedient to do so. Say, to protect someone you loved?'

Beneath his lashes his eyes were cold as shards of emerald, without a shred of emotion, stripping her of all her defences.

'I don't know what you mean,' she said, all sorts of wild scenarios chasing themselves through her brain. What had he done...?

'Try answering the question.'

'I'm not a very good liar,' she said, her mouth dry.

'Yet you lied about driving the car that killed Olivia Saywell.'

It was a nightmare, twisted, nothing making sense. She whispered, 'What do you mean? How did you know——? I did drive it—and I said so.'

'And yet you say you're not a good liar.' Those implacable eyes filled with a black anger. As she shrank back he said between his teeth, 'Olivia is—*was* my stepsister. She died after writing me a letter. In it she said that you and your cousin and she went to a party, and that while you were there he got drunk. But he insisted on driving. She said that she was slightly drunk herself and so tired that she went to sleep as soon as she got into the car, but she can remember that in spite of what you stated at the inquest he was behind the wheel. You didn't put her seatbelt on, although you remembered to put your own on, both of you. And he drove off the cliff. But you and he lied, you said that it was you behind the wheel. Because you were more sober than he was, by the time the police got there to breath-test you you were below the limit.'

She became dimly conscious that breathing hurt. Pinned by those icily merciless eyes, she swallowed, having to force down the lump that threatened to choke her before she could say in a trembling voice, 'I've never heard such rubbish in all my life! Chris wasn't drunk; he'd taken medication for hayfever, and because of it he couldn't drive. Of course I drove. And we got her seatbelt on, although she screamed and shrieked and hit me in the face while I was doing it. She must have undone it later.' Her lips trembled. 'I should have watched her more closely—do you think I haven't wondered time after time if she'd still be alive if I'd checked?'

'Why would she lie to me?' he demanded with an inexorable harshness that terrified her. 'She knew she was going to kill herself. Why the hell did she say that if it wasn't true?'

She put a hand to her throbbing head, frowning, trying to make sense of what had happened. 'I don't know. It doesn't make sense.'

'Unless it was true, and you were shielding this cousin of yours.'

'It wasn't true, it was a pack of lies!' She shouted the words at him, her voice breaking with anguish. 'I drove, damn you. I'll tell you who was drunk, or high, or whatever it was, and that was your precious stepsister!'

He looked at her, his face bleak and coldly chiselled. 'I know. She rang me, but I was overseas. When I got home her message was on the answerphone. She said you were all drunk, and she wanted me to come and pick her up.'

'She lied,' she spat, terrified because she could see that he wasn't going to believe her, and there was no way she could counter Olivia's malice. 'Don't you think that if there had been anything like that it would have come out at the inquest?'

He said with an icy contempt, 'It was two hours later before you managed to crawl to the road. The police did test you for alcohol, but all traces would have gone by then. I notice you haven't much tolerance for it.'

'I'd had two glasses of wine early on in the evening,' she said tonelessly, realising that it had all been a sham. He hadn't ever wanted her, or no more than a man could want any convenient woman. He had made love to her with a cruel cynicism that was going to break her heart when she had time to appreciate what he had done. 'I wasn't drunk. We went over the bank because Olivia woke and decided she wanted to drive. I tried to calm her down, but she got hysterical and grabbed the wheel.'

'But you said nothing about this.'

She said defensively, 'Chris was in love with her. And she—how could I tell anyone what she had done when she—when she was——'

'Say it,' he said savagely. 'She was a cripple.'

Kathy drew a deep shuddering breath. 'I couldn't hurt her any more than she had been hurt! And the police agreed that whoever stole the lantern from the barrier was responsible for our going over. If I hadn't slowed down to see what had happened to the road she might not have woken.'

'It sounds,' he sneered, 'altogether too convenient. *Just* before you came along some idiot stole the lantern from the barriers. *Just* at that moment when you were coming up to the road subsidence she woke and grabbed the wheel. And presumably *just* before that she had released her safety-belt. Too many justs, Kathy.' He made her name a sneer, an obscenity.

She stared at him, her eyes a muddy brown, all life and colour drained away. 'So you believed her and you decided to exact a little revenge,' she said tonelessly. 'And like a fool I gave you the perfect opportunity. I'm surprised you didn't make love to me first. Wouldn't that have made your revenge that much sweeter?'

He shrugged. 'Not my style. I don't seduce. Besides,' he added cruelly, 'I don't really find you very attractive. Too juvenile.'

He couldn't have settled on a more hurtful insult. She whitened as though he had struck her, but she had enough self-control to hold back the tears. Raggedly, she persisted, 'Whatever feelings you had for Olivia, you must have known what sort of person she was. Untrustworthy——'

'She never lied to me,' he said with a cold-blooded indifference that iced over her emotions. 'Never. That's how I know she was telling the truth. And, yes, I did decide that you needed to be punished. You lied to protect your cousin. Morally, you are just as much at fault as he is. So I found you, and I must admit it was ridiculously easy to coax you into falling in love with me. But don't worry, I have no intention of seducing you. When your cousin finally gets around to marrying you you'll still be a virgin.'

She stared at him, her face registering complete bewilderment. 'What are you talking about? Chris is my cousin, for heaven's sake!'

'And cousins marry. Olivia told me that he was waiting for you to grow up; she was just a stopgap.'

She got to her feet suddenly, saying passionately, 'I don't have to listen to such sick lies! Chris is like a very dear brother, and he loved Olivia. Why do you think he put up with her wildness, her cruelty? She was a selfish, treacherous bitch, but for all that I wouldn't have wanted her to become a paraplegic, or to kill herself, and Chris wanted to marry her, even after the accident. She refused, and banned him from seeing her. She broke his heart.'

His hand clamped around her wrist, holding her still. 'Hold it,' he commanded, his voice steel-hard. 'Where do you think you're going?'

'I'm not staying here.'

His eyes were flat and unwinking, green slivers of ice lit from behind by the fury he had well under control. 'Do you think so?' he mocked, watching her tormented face with disdain. 'You haven't had your punishment, yet, Kathy. You came up to stay for three weeks with me.'

She looked at him with undisguised horror. 'You said that—you said I——'

'I said I didn't want you,' he finished for her, cruelly underlining his statement. 'I don't. And I won't touch you. But I'm going to make you suffer just a little for the farrago of lies you've just spouted. Yes, Olivia was wild and selfish and passionate, but she loved your cousin, and his treachery killed her. She truly thought he loved her; she was sure that this time she had found a man who wouldn't betray her. You think you love me, so you can go through a little of the pain she endured when he no longer came to see her at the hospital.' She opened her mouth and he said ferociously, 'I know all about it, damn you! I was overseas at the time, I couldn't get back, but her mother was with her and she said she used to weep for hours.'

Dazed, her mind thrown so completely out of kilter that she thought she might be going mad, she said wearily, 'I'm not staying here. I'll walk down to Kaeo if I have to, but——'

His fingers tightened painfully around her wrist. 'You're not going anywhere.'

'That's kidnapping,' she said, white-lipped.

He smiled unpleasantly. 'So it is. And when you go to the police I'll tell them we've just had a lovers' quarrel. I might even leak it to the Press. I'm sure those puritan parents of yours would hate to see their daughter's name splashed across the scandal sheets. As well, I'll make sure that your beloved Chris loses his job and never gets another one in New Zealand. I've already pulled strings and I'm afraid he's going to find that his career path's about to take a sudden dive.'

She was so pale she couldn't lose more colour, but she whipped up enough defiance to say, 'You can't do that.'

'Care to put it to the test?'

No, and he knew it. For a long moment her aching eyes skimmed the merciless features of the man she had thought she loved. He wasn't bluffing. She didn't know whether he could make good his threat, but she couldn't risk his trying.

In a low, defeated voice she said, 'I hate you. You're wicked and cruel, but most of all you're gullible, because you can't see that your adored stepsister, a woman you admit was selfish and spoiled and wild, was just taking you for a ride.'

'Nice try,' he said, his mouth twisting in a parody of a smile. 'I don't think I've ever been called gullible before. Oh, you make it sound very convincing. I admire that touching little sob in your voice. I might even believe you, only I come back to one thing. Olivia had no reason to lie to me. By the time she told me all this, she knew she was going to kill herself. Why should she fill me with a pack of lies?'

'Perhaps she had a nice taste for revenge too,' she said in a hard, curt voice that hid her agony of heart and spirit. 'And, of course, there was the fact that both Chris and I could walk, and we were the people who had indirectly taken that freedom from her.'

'You little bitch,' he said between his teeth. 'If I had had any inclination to believe your protestations of innocence, I certainly wouldn't now.'

'You couldn't,' she said sadly. 'You've been brainwashed. You can let me go now, I won't try to escape.'

After a hard survey he released her wrist, commanding casually, 'Sit down and eat.'

'I can't.' Nausea made her swallow.

'Starving yourself is not going to change my mind. If necessary I'll force food down your throat.'

The softly spoken threat convinced her. With trembling hands she picked up the implements and began to eat, chewing food that had turned dry and tasteless, like Dead Sea fruit in her mouth.

He refined the cruelty, speaking coolly and calmly of various things, mocking her with a parody of the conversation she had come to depend on. And he wasn't content with that. He insisted she answer, listening with derisive courtesy to her shaking voice, pretending that nothing had changed.

Three weeks of this, she thought in anguish. She could not bear it.

After dinner he left her in silence while he read. The food she had forced down seemed to be choking her, but she knew that it was black unhappiness. Three weeks.

The words danced before her eyes, blurring together as she lowered her head and fought back the tears. *She would not let him see her cry.* He thought she was juvenile, stupid, easily seduced, and he was right, he had been right from the start, but she would not cry. That would be the ultimate humiliation.

'Time for bed,' he said, startling her so that she flinched. As if he hadn't noticed, he added, 'You have the bathroom first.'

On stiff legs she went into the tiny spartan room and showered, trying to wash the unclean feeling from her skin, then made the usual preparations for the night. In her bag was the prescription she had got from the doctor; the tears burned in her throat as she stuffed it so far down that she wouldn't need to see it again until she was back in Auckland.

Her nightgown was one she had made with such high hopes, a floating summery thing with small gold and green flowers on a cream background. The material had been expensive but in her stupidity she had thought it worth it. Not exactly transparent, it was not opaque, either. Suffering the humiliation of the betrayed, she walked into the bedroom, knowing that through the fine cotton he could see her long golden legs, and the slender feminine outline of her breasts and waist and hips.

He looked at her without emotion. 'Sit on the end of the bed while I shower,' he said. 'Where I can keep an eye on you.'

She obeyed, sitting straight, her eyes fixed on to the wall opposite, blanking out her thoughts as she traced a faint crack across the smooth surface. When he came back in her face burned with unruly colour, for he was clad only in briefs; after the first shocked glance she stared intently at her hands.

'Into bed,' he said.

Wordlessly she got in, pulling the sheet around her throat, closing her eyes. But the tilting of the springs on the opposite side made them fly open. 'No!' she said breathlessly, scrabbling for the side of the bed.

His hand snaked out and caught her arm, clamping her to the mattress. 'I have no intention of making love to you,' he said coldly, 'but I'm not going to sleep on the floor.'

'I'll sleep on the floor,' she said breathlessly, hating the begging note in her voice but unable to conceal it.

'You will not. I want you where I can keep an eye on you.'

'I won't try to run away,' she pleaded, her face hidden in the pillow, her body rigid with shock and rejection. 'I promise I won't.'

'But we know you lie,' he said softly, pleasantly, his hand tightening for a moment before he let her go. 'Settle down. Believe me, I want to touch you as little as you want to touch me.'

'André, please,' she whispered.

'Please what? Please let me go? No. Please make love to me? Well, if you persuade me——'

'No!' She shrank back, dumbly revealing her revulsion.

'Then lie still and go to sleep,' he said coldly. 'And remember, I sleep very lightly, and, just in case it occurs to you, the car is disabled.'

She didn't think she would sleep at all, her body at war with her mind and her emotions, tormented by the sensuality he had woken, betrayed and humiliated, but the stress of the day had worn her out and before she realised it she was asleep.

The nightmare came abruptly, as it always did, catapulting her into awareness with a vicious realism that opened her mouth in a silent scream. The road snaked in front of her, the tyres on Chris's car humming, rain glistening silver in the lights. She knew what was going to happen and she tried to stop the car, her will forcing her useless hands, calling out to her lax, immobile body to stop, stop...

And then the moment when she realised the barrier ahead hid a gaping hole in the road, and the slow slide as more of the tarmac disappeared, the shocking squeal as part of the barrier scraped along the side of the car...

She heard Olivia's scream, felt the scratch of rocks and metal, the heavy thuds, the awful tearing sounds as the greedy rocks tore at the vehicle. And there, in front of her, the door springing open and Olivia screaming as she was flung out, her mouth open, her face white in the darkness...

In reality she remembered nothing beyond Olivia's frenzied grab at the wheel but her over-active brain supplied the details her eyes had missed, and every time it got worse, the anticipation more excruciating, the details more vivid. She longed for the unconsciousness that followed, the pain in the head that signalled numbness.

But this time there was no pain, no blessed slide into oblivion. Someone was shaking her with strong hands, someone was saying her name in a flat deadly monotone. She woke with a gasping sob, and burst into tears, turning her head into the chest of the man who had woken her, her heart thundering unbearably in her ears.

His arms were warm and strong around her, his chest broad and comforting; for the fraction of a second that it took her to regain her memory it was like a safe homecoming.

Then she remembered, and froze, before wrenching herself away to her side of the bed. Using the back of one hand to wipe away the tears, she groped under the pillow for her handkerchief with the other, found it and used it, keeping her face covered.

'What the hell was that about?' He sounded shaken.

In a croaky little voice she said stiffly, 'I'm sorry, it was just a nightmare.'

'You were yelling Olivia's name.'

'Yes.'

Silence and then he said, 'I see. Do you have them often?'

'Not as often as I used to.' She blew her nose and slid back down under the sheet. After Auckland's humid nights the air up here was cool, almost crisp, and she was beginning to shiver. 'I'm sorry I woke you,' she said formally, ridiculously. 'Goodnight.'

This time she didn't get to sleep. For hours she lay listening to the sound of the waterfall as it plunged over the bank, and the voice of a morepork calling forlornly for his mate. She heard the regular breathing of the man beside her, resenting his effortless slide into oblivion with a ferocity that surprised her, and she had never felt so alone in all her life.

It set a pattern for the other nights, and the days, she spent as his prisoner. There were no further nightmares, but she was forced to lie and listen to him sleep, and during the day he made her accompany him wherever he went: swimming in the pool, hiking through bush that he knew like the back of his hand, lying in the sun. He made her eat, he made her sleep with him, and whenever his eyes fell on her she shivered at the implacable disciplined bitterness she saw there. She began to hate the sound of her own name, used with a fine edge of contempt; when she got away, she thought one day, she would never answer to Kathy again. She would call herself Kate.

She knew she woke after each lonely painful night with deeper shadows under her eyes, and that she was losing weight. It seemed bitterly unfair that the weather was perfect—lazy, drowsy days punctuated by blissfully cool nights. Perfect for lovers. Her smile was rare and bitter. She hated him, but the desires he had woken ate away at her self-respect in a forbidden need.

One day he went out and began to chop out a large clump of gorse that was starting to encroach on to the grass. She lay on the terrace and watched the rhythmic movement of his arms as he swung the slasher. There was something demonic, ferociously personal about the way he worked, his sleek body blazing with energy and force, as though the gorse was a hated enemy.

With drooping lashes she stared at him, her mind settling into the black fog of apathy she no longer tried to fight. After a couple of hours she went into the bedroom. Exhaustion warred with common sense; she said aloud, weakly, 'Just for a few minutes...'

But when she awoke it was in the quiet golden evening to see him watching her, his face immobile. He looked tired, his features drawn into a grim mask. His shirt was stained with sweat, and as, horrified, she stared mutely at him he wiped the back of his hand across his forehead.

'Were you waiting for me?' Each word was cool and controlled, but in his eyes there burned a secret flame.

'No,' she whispered.

'If you don't want me to join you you had better get up,' he said quite pleasantly.

She scrambled out as though all the devils in hell were after her.

The following day, six days after he had shattered her dream of paradise, a car bumped slowly down the track. Even as Kathy recognised it, she couldn't believe that it was Libby's little Honda.

André's eyes narrowed and into his expression came that knowing challenge that she had noticed before when he looked at Libby.

She said quietly, 'I'm going back with her.'

'I think not,' he said, equally quietly. 'Think of your cousin.'

'Chris,' she said intensely, 'is going to have to take care of himself. I can't stay here any longer.'

'Why? Because you still want me?'

She turned on him with a pitiful attempt at dignity, her mouth trembling at his fierce beauty, the masculine attraction that hid so much cruelty. 'As you said, I'm young. I'll grow up.'

And she turned and walked across the grass.

Libby climbed out of her car, smiling, yet subtly on edge. 'Hi,' she called. 'I thought I'd come and see how things were getting on.'

And Kathy said, 'Good, because I want you to take me home.'

CHAPTER FIVE

LIBBY stared at them both, her startled gaze moving from one to the other. 'What's happened?' she asked.

André said, 'Nothing,' at the same time as Kathy said, 'Lib, André has been holding out on us. He's Olivia Saywell's stepbrother.'

Libby's gaze flew to André's hard, handsome face. *'What?'*

'Yes,' he said, showing his teeth in a wolf's smile. 'Did you know her?'

'Yes,' Libby said tonelessly. 'Not very well. But well enough to know that when she spoke of you it was not as a brother. I thought you were her lover.'

His face darkened. 'Nonsense.'

'No,' Libby said slowly, darting a sharp look at Kathy's stony face. 'It was not nonsense.' She hesitated, then went on in a brusque voice, 'Olivia told everyone what a wonderful lover you were, and, given the opportunity, would describe your lovemaking in graphic detail. Ask Kathy. I warned her when you first started going out with her that according to Olivia you had been one of her lovers. Didn't I, Kathy?'

Kathy nodded. She felt curiously exhausted, almost dissociated from them, as though something had snapped and now nothing could worry her.

André swore. 'She was my stepsister, damn it!'

'It clearly didn't stop her from wanting you.' Libby was not intimidated by his cold fury.

His eyes never left Kathy's face but the question was addressed to Libby. 'Were you around the night Olivia was injured?'

88

'Yes. I was going to go back with them, but other things intervened.'

André shot a triumphant glance at Kathy, standing white and still beside him. She shivered, for it was filled with a terrible triumph. 'And who drove?' he asked silkily.

Libby's brows lifted. 'Kathy did.'

He was very still, like a great beast ready to pounce. 'Did you actually see her?'

'Yes. I helped them both get Olivia into the car.'

In a calm voice he said, 'You're lying.'

'No.'

'Chris drove,' he said evenly. 'He was drunk. And so was Kathy.'

'Wait a minute.' Libby's gaze slid from Kathy's still white face to André's harsh avenging countenance. 'What do you mean, Kathy was drunk? That's ridiculous. She had a couple of drinks with dinner, that's all.'

André said levelly, 'And I suppose Chris was perfectly sober, too.'

'He'd taken hayfever medication. He seemed OK, but he refused to drive.' Libby gave him a long unflinching look. 'I'll tell you who wasn't fit to drive, and that was your precious sister.'

He stood very still, like a leashed tiger. Kathy's heart jumped. She looked pleadingly at Libby, but the older woman was still watching André, her mouth compressed.

'She was,' she continued deliberately, 'drunk, and she'd had something else, pills or something. She was as high as a kite and spoiling for a fight. Even before Kathy got the car going she had refused to put on her seatbelt. When they argued about it, she snatched at the wheel. Then she got hysterical, screaming that she couldn't breathe, it was too tight, and she wouldn't wear the damned belt. Between us we managed to get her into it, and believe me, I've never come closer to smacking a woman's face. She was raving, in a vicious, foul-mouthed rage.'

Her eyes swept André's face, softening a little as they caught Kathy's dull gaze. She ended flatly, with a cruelty that astonished her friend, 'I wasn't surprised at the accident, although if anyone had to be hurt it was just as well it was her, and not the innocent parties.'

André showed his teeth. 'You're lying,' he said again, a threat so implicit in his stance and his words that Kathy stirred, ready to step between them.

Libby looked at him. 'I am telling the truth. Which, by the sound of it, is more than Olivia ever did.'

'She told me,' he said, still in those lethally quiet tones, 'the night before she died, that Chris was drunk, that he and Kathy had conspired to keep the fact that he was driving from the police. Why would she tell me that, if it wasn't true?'

'Because she wanted to punish us,' Kathy said unexpectedly, her voice dragging with tiredness. 'She told us that she would get even if it was the last thing she did.'

Libby forgotten, he turned on her. But this time, instead of the hatred and contempt she had come to know so well, there was desperation behind the ferocious mask of his features. 'If what Libby says is true, what the hell did she have to punish you for?'

Damningly Libby said, 'Because Kathy is pretty; she can attract men, make love. When Olivia came out of her coma all *she* had was Chris. Her down-market stud, she called him. She was so snobbish, she didn't realise that he was worth twenty of the men she boasted about sleeping with. Poor Chris still wanted to marry her but she didn't want him. I don't think she ever did. Olivia had to have a man to sleep with or she didn't think she was alive. Other women have suffered just as badly as Olivia, and managed to make something of their lives, but she had no reserves, nothing but her looks and her body and the animal vitality that made her so desirable.

When they were taken from her she had nothing left to live for. I've always thought that her death was inevitable; she'd have committed suicide as soon as the drink and the drugs and the sex started to take toll of her looks and she couldn't get the men she wanted.'

'All right,' he said harshly, goaded but apparently not surprised by this dispassionate summation of his step-sister's character. 'So she was self-destructive—we all know that. But why did she tell me a farrago of lies?'

'I'd say she wanted to punish those who she decided, in her twisted mind, had taken everything she valued about herself from her.' Libby's eyes met André's, giving no quarter. 'No doubt,' she finished tellingly, 'she knew enough of your taste for revenge to guess that you wouldn't rest until you'd done as much damage as you could.'

'But I let her down,' he said half beneath his breath.

Kathy almost cried out. Beneath the teak tan his skin was white, drawn tightly over the underlying structure so that the hawk features were like a mask. The green eyes were opaque and dull, but she could see the torment in them before he closed them for a second.

'I told her that I was no longer prepared to step in and rescue her,' he said with dreadful irony, 'because the psychiatrist I had consulted suggested that one of the reasons she refused to take responsibility for her actions was that I had always done so for her. So I went overseas without making arrangements to see that she couldn't get into trouble. And I compounded my stupidity by believing her and letting my own guilt persuade me into avenging her.'

He turned and walked across the grass towards the darkness of the bush, moving still with lithe panther grace but for once without the blazing masculine vitality. He looked as though he was completely turned in on himself. Kathy had thought she hated him, but at that moment all she could feel was a deep sympathy. If ever a man was in hell, André was.

'What a bloody woman,' Libby said angrily. 'Not content with mucking up her own life, she had to leave a legacy that ruined André's and yours, and, I'm very much afraid, Chris's too.'

How much had she guessed? Too much, by the compassionate look. Kathy put a hand to her neck, pushing against tense muscles, averting her eyes.

'It's all right,' Libby went on, discerning her thoughts too accurately. 'I won't ask. But, honestly, what a bitch! To lie and lie and lie again, even when she knew she was going to commit suicide...'

Kathy shivered. 'She was mad,' she said with conviction.

'Perhaps, although I think she was more evil than mad. God, what a mess! What are you going to do?'

Kathy drew back into herself. 'Nothing,' she said quietly.

Libby sighed. 'I feel like an absolute swine.' Her mouth stretched in an ironically mirthless smile. 'I'd better confess. I've had a hankering for André ever since I saw him that first time. He knows, too. He's too bloody clever by half. To be brutally honest I came up here because I couldn't stay away, but all this has given me an extremely nasty taste in my mouth. You'd better come with me now.'

'I can't.'

Libby looked at her with horrified astonishment, but she was still watching the place where André had disappeared into the trees.

'You said you wanted to leave,' Libby pointed out without much hope of being attended to.

'I can't leave him now, not when he's in such pain. He loved Olivia, in spite of everything.' Kathy's voice deepened on a poignant note. 'I wonder what she had that made men love her, even when she was so awful?'

'All she had were flashy good looks and the morals of an alley cat. Kathy, don't stay here. He won't want you, he's the sort of man who prefers to lick his wounds in private.'

Kathy shivered, but said quietly, 'It doesn't matter, I can't just walk out. There are things I want to say—I'd like to finish it properly.'

'And you don't want to leave him when he's so unhappy,' Libby said shrewdly. She didn't give up easily, trying to persuade her to go, but Kathy was adamant, and finally the older woman left, saying, 'Look, I'll stay overnight in the pub at Kaeo. If you need me, promise you'll ring. Promise?'

'He won't be violent, Lib, but OK, I promise.' She didn't tell her that there was no telephone in the house.

In the heavy silence Libby left behind her Kathy went quietly about the house tidying up, longing for something difficult to do that would take her mind off what had happened. Ironic to think that the truth she had so longed for had come with Libby. And even more ironic to realise that in the end André had believed Libby, whereas he had never believed her. If anything revealed just how empty their relationship was, it was that.

The house was eerily quiet. Kathy watched the sun go down behind the hills and made dinner, but he didn't emerge from the trees and she couldn't eat any herself. She had thought that when he finally knew the truth she would be so relieved and triumphant; now all she could feel was an empty sorrow for all the anguish and the stupid, unnecessary suffering.

For André had suffered, was still suffering. She had always known that his perfidy was rooted in the depths of his pain and his remorse for failing the woman he considered to be his sister.

Finally, when it had been dark for some hours, she went to bed and lay for endless time with her eyes open, staring at the unseen ceiling while thoughts chased themselves like caged animals around her mind.

Sleep came subtly, so that it was with a shock that she realised she was not alone in the room. She woke with a heavily beating heart, as though she could sense the menace in the man who stood by the bed staring down at her.

'André?' she said softly.

'Were you expecting someone else? Brent Sheridan, perhaps?'

A last foolish hope, unborn, unrecognised until that moment, died. Nothing had changed. 'No,' she said steadily. 'What do you want?'

He laughed, a dreadful sound. 'What do I want? Well, that's a question. I want quite a few things. For starters, I'd like the past year to be wiped off the record, but that's not going to happen, is it?'

'No.'

'So I'm going to have to live with the mess I've made of everything.' He spoke meditatively, but she lay very still, for in his voice there was an anger made all the more intense by the stringent self-control he was exerting. 'Why did you stay here, Kathy?'

'I thought—I thought we had things to say to each other. I thought you might need me.'

'Why would I need you?' he sneered. 'Do you want your pound of flesh? An apology? Or the passion I denied you when I decided to make you pay for what I thought you had done to my treacherous, malicious bitch of a stepsister? I must be bloody dim! I knew what she was like, but because she had never lied to me before I believed her.'

Her skin tightened. 'Loyalty is not a sin.'

'Stupidity and vanity and lust are. Oh, when I went looking for you I was hot for vengeance but I doubt very much whether I'd have kept on with this plan if I hadn't stared across a stuffy room one hot night in an Auckland suburb and seen Jezebel dancing.'

'I am not a Jezebel,' she returned quietly. 'I'm just an ordinary woman. Stupid. Too stupid to realise that all of it was lies.'

He sighed. 'Lies? No, it wasn't all lies. But you know that, don't you? Do you think a man can fake the sort of response I felt that night?' He sat down on the side of the bed, turning towards her. 'Or the physical response whenever we kiss? Women can pretend, but not men, Kathy. I didn't lie when I said I wanted you.'

And he had never said anything else. In a strange way he had been truthful. It was her own naïveté that had lied. She lay very still, her breath caught in her throat. He had been drinking; she could smell the faint odour of whisky on him. Not a lot. Just enough, perhaps, to take the edge off that rigid self-control.

'I knew that you had to be punished,' he said, still in that soft, deadly tone. 'You, and the man who loved you. She told me that that was why Chris turned her down, you know; because he loved you. She was just a body to keep him warm while he waited for you to grow up.'

'Chris is my cousin!' she whispered, sickened by this further evidence of Olivia's malice. 'She was mad.'

'Yes, I'm afraid she was. But when I saw you, dancing with that witch's smile on your face, as lithe and sinuous as Mélisande, I realised why poor, egotistical, self-destructive Olivia didn't have a show. First cousins have married before today, you know. And I could quite believe that Chris wanted you. Hell, every man in that room wanted you! Everything that Olivia longed to be, tried so hard to be, you were: young, and so beautiful, totally unconscious of your power. I watched you dancing and I knew that I could lose my soul wanting you, in spite of the fact that you were a liar, in spite of everything.

I wanted you so much that I would have died to have you.'

She made a broken little noise of pain, chilled by his soft, cold laughter. 'And you felt the same. I saw it happen to you too. You looked up at me and those strange cat's eyes darkened with an awareness you couldn't hide.' His hand touched her cheek, pushed back a tress of reddish-copper hair. The fingers were cold and shaking very slightly.

Kathy said quietly, 'André, it's over. It's all over. I can't see any good in rehashing the whole miserable affair.'

His fingers had been moving slowly across her face, caressing her cheeks, tracing the hollows beneath the sweep of bone, coming inevitably to her mouth. 'No. I suppose you want to go.'

'Yes. I'll go tomorrow morning. And I think that tonight I'd better sleep on the sofa.'

'So it was just a crush,' he said softly as his hand cupped the back of her neck, holding her still. 'It had to be, of course, and God knows, nothing I've done has helped you develop any more lasting emotion, has it?'

'If we had fallen in love,' she said with sadness, 'it might have been different. But you despised me, and you took good care that I never got to know you. I'm sorry.'

'You're sorry?' He sounded incredulous and angry. 'What for? For being available when I wanted an instrument of revenge on your cousin?'

His hands moved, pulled her up into his arms. 'I watched you this last week,' he said thickly. 'So bloody lovely, so innocently provocative, and so unhappy, and I told myself that you deserved it because you had lied, you had sheltered the man who killed Olivia, she was dead and you and your cousin were alive. I must be a little naïve myself, because it seemed to me that no one on the brink of death would lie. And she had never lied to me before, poor driven Olivia, who had lied all her life. She tricked me into taking revenge. By believing her I threw away any chance of finding out exactly what it is that I feel for you, that you feel for me. Except for this...'

His mouth was sweet, tasting faintly of whisky but soft and seducing, and she, who had been convinced that her desire for him was dead, was horrified at the wave of sensation that swamped her.

Unconsciously her lips moulded to his, parting slightly, accepting the sudden thrust of his tongue, and then it was all over, the barricades she had built so carefully, with so much pain and effort, swept away under the surge of emotions and sensations, inextricably mixed, sweet as sugar, potent as the rawest spirit, so that she was mindless and helpless before it.

At last he lifted his head, but it was only to breathe her name in a shaken voice before he kissed her again, and this time there was little gentleness. She didn't mind, she craved the passion she sensed he was holding under such restraint. The bitter week, the disillusion and anguish seeped away; here in this room, in this bed, in the friendly darkness, they came together as equals, lost in a passion that had been long in the making.

'André,' she breathed in an aching voice.

'Do you like that? Do you want more?' His voice was deep and rough and shocking, but even more shocking was her response, the way she held her mouth up, following the cruel length of his with the tip of her tongue until he shuddered and crushed her beneath him once more, drinking her sweetness as though he could lose himself in the honeyed tide of desire. If she had any thought of stopping him it was washed away in the scalding response he evoked with his practised hands and mouth.

'Yes,' he said deeply, his voice rough and harsh. 'I knew it could be like this, I knew it right from the start, and the knowledge made me cruel because I had to fight myself as well as you. Every time I saw your sweet face I saw Olivia, broken in her pain, and I knew that I wanted you as I never wanted anyone else. I wonder why? Some cosmic joke, I suppose. What does the Bible say? "Vengeance is mine; I will repay, saith the Lord." I wish I'd taken more notice of it.'

She wanted only to ease the anguish she heard in every word, pain and torment and bitter self-contempt. 'Hush,' she said softly, her hands on either side of the lean, drawn face. 'Don't expect yourself to be perfect. Everybody makes mistakes, André.'

He stared down into the sweet gravity of her face, his eyes for once clear, lit from behind by a glow she recognised as hunger, stark and merciless. 'Yes,' he said with an odd inflexion. 'Everyone does, and I think this is going to be another one, but I'm damned if I can summon the resolution to walk out of that door.'

His mouth was almost cruel, the kiss that of a conqueror taking a slave girl on the field of battle. But the moment the soft sound of protest left her lips he broke off the kiss, and when he nuzzled her throat and the piercingly sensitive spot just below her ear there was nothing but seduction in his touch.

Kathy knew that she should resist. She too understood that if they surrendered to this passion, sprung fullblown between them the first time their eyes met, she would pay for it for the rest of her life. But like him she was unable to withstand it. Her breath sighed out from her lungs, yielding the field, and he laughed with the arrogant possession of a man who knew that he had won and pulled her on to the bed, sliding down with her beneath the sheet.

There was no moon, but the night borrowed enough light from the stars to reveal the outlines of her body beneath the thin cotton nightgown she wore. Primal tides of sensation surged through her as she felt the fire of his gaze on her; she had always been modest, except when music broke through her reticence, and now that same fierce exultation tightened her muscles and ran like hot wires through every cell in her body. Her eyes gleamed, her full, kiss-stung lips parted in a slight, ancient female smile, one of recognition and satisfaction, of promise and the forbidden, savage excitement of the perilous unknown.

Without humour, he laughed just below his breath as his lean fingers moved to the silken skin at the base of her throat. Teasing her, touching her with flirtatious wilfulness, he stroked across her shoulders. And when she moaned slightly and arched, her arms rising to pull him close, he caught her hands in his and pulled them above her head, holding her open to his gaze, shielded only by the thin cotton gown.

'No,' she muttered.

'Yes.'

'I want——'

His smile was wicked. 'Haven't you yet realised that it is what I want that matters, you little siren? You know what it does to me when you smile at me like that, offering me all the proscribed delights of paradise, sinfully wanton and yet a necessity more vital than breathing. I wonder if you'll cloy after a while, if I'll become sated even with you. I think I'm going to enjoy finding out.'

He bent his head and touched the pleading, aching mound of her breast with his tongue, smiling into the cotton as the nipple peaked against his mouth. 'Yes,' he murmured, 'you have signs too, hidden better than a man's, but there for those with eyes to see. Do you want more than that, my sweet siren, my innocent Delilah? You'll have to wait. I don't intend to hurry with you—I've waited too long.'

Her protest at his insulting remarks died at the further touch of his tongue. Fire streaked from her breasts, gathered in a conflagration at her loins, drove every thought from her mind but the desperate need to assuage this primeval anguish. Unable to break free from his grip, she found relief from the taut hunger by arching pleadingly towards him, impelled by instincts as old as womankind, as fresh as that very night.

He laughed again, and his mouth closed hotly over her breast, the strong suckling easing her craving a little. But when he lifted his head she realised that it had only exacerbated the hunger that gripped her at the junction of her body. Her skin was pulled tight, heated and unbearably sensitive. She ached with new and unknown sensations. Again her muscles tightened, her voice sobbing over words she didn't recognise, words that tumbled out without volition.

'Yes,' he said soothingly, and let her hands go. Free at last, they clutched beseechingly at him, but he said, 'Undress for me, Kathy. Show me how beautiful you are with the starlight silvering your body.'

She hesitated, meeting the compelling fire in his gaze with an odd helplessness, then slowly her hands found the hem of the nightgown and she pulled it over her head, wriggling free of its clinging folds. She didn't need the harsh indrawn breath to tell her of his reaction; she read it in the sudden stillness that gripped him.

'Oh, you are beautiful,' he said harshly. 'As beautiful as a star, as a flower, as a dream. Now, take my clothes off, Kathy. All through these long weeks I've consoled myself with the fantasy of feeling your hands on me. I can't wait any longer.'

Tentatively at first she reached out, bemused by his taut stillness. His breath was torn from him, a quick, sharp, painful hiss as she touched the buttons on his shirt. Emboldened, she slid the small discs free, and pulled the cloth back. She had seen him often enough without his shirt to know what lay beneath, the smooth, swelling curves of muscle overlying the lean, hard contours of his body, the primitive feral grace, power and predation combined in a heady mixture of male sensuality.

Always before she had been careful not to let him see her watching, but now she feasted her eyes, her hand outstretched to trace the faint scrolls of hair that decorated him in a pattern as masculine as it was stimulating. He sat still, not a muscle moving, and she glanced up. One glance from those glittering green eyes reassured her; his mouth might be compressed into a thin straight line, but a muscle flicking in his jaw revealed how close he was to some unknown edge.

Kathy did what she had wanted to do so badly, and touched the tiny male nipples. Like hers they stiffened, but even as she rejoiced in the power of her femininity an answering streak of fire proved how vulnerable she was.

'Yes,' he said, half beneath his breath. 'It cuts both ways, little sensualist. The power I cede to you is matched by my power over you. Kiss me.'

Dazed by sensation, she leaned forward and put her mouth to his chest, suckling him as he had her. To her incredulous excitement he groaned, the sound shattering in the still room, his excitement a palpable force in the cool air.

The fire in her body began to build, combining with an ache that reminded her of the time she had influenza, when she had tossed in bed for days. But this strange restlessness was not due to a virus; it came from deep within her, was rooted in her body and blood, a legacy from the primeval beginnings of the human race, the imperative to surrender and reproduce.

A warning fought to break free from the hazy hunger that held her captive; she drew in a deep jagged breath and leaned her cheek against the hard wall of his torso, fighting to recognise the threat she so dimly discerned, but he whispered, 'Oh, God, darling, don't stop now,' and the last spark of common sense slid beneath a tide of sensation.

Her hands fumbled with his belt buckle; he groaned a laugh, and pressed her fingers against the hard bulge beneath, refusing to let her pull free.

'See what you do to me,' he muttered. 'Never before, Kathy, not like this. Not ever like this, as though I'll die if I don't have you...'

His voice faded as he stood up and with a few swift brutal movements divested himself of his trousers. Her mouth dried. Seen like that, a male animal in all his pride, he was awe-inspiring, and fearsome too.

Then he slid down beside her on the bed, and the heated slick of his skin banished the moment of panic. With a soft sob she turned towards him, knowing like him only that if she didn't have him she would die, ravished by the powerful command of instincts that were now paramount.

His mouth was hot and rapacious, his hands unbearably skilful as they teased her sensitised skin, until finally, after stretched, tense moments when her frustration was so great that she cried out with it, the lean, strong fingers searched out the centre of her desire. Her gasp, and the sudden involuntary arcing of her body, made him laugh softly.

With a swiftness that should have terrified her he was over her, her wrists imprisoned in his strong hands by her shoulders, his body smooth and sinuous as a great cat's. She opened half-closed eyes and looked up into his face, her eyes widening fearfully as she saw the age-old need take command of him, stripping his expression of everything but a fierce, demanding hunger, impersonal in its relentless strength.

For a moment she stiffened, and then he lowered himself in a smooth thrust, taking her without thought for her inexperience, completely lost to anything but his own hunger.

She cried out again in shock. Expecting pain, she had felt nothing but a sensation of impalement, of the tissues and surfaces of her body shifting to accommodate him. It was then, lost in the essential rightness of this, that she realised why she had refused to go with Libby.

His heart thundered in his chest, deafening her. For a moment he was still, until his body began to move again. Sensations burst out through her; she forgot the shock and the novelty, forgot everything but the necessity to respond to this wonderful compulsion. Her hips moved, slowly at first, and then with increasing speed; the desire that had been gathering in every cell in her body grew to unbearable proportions until she was lost to everything but her body and his, the elemental combination that led to this ecstatic junction.

And then, like a storm that had been brewing for hours, rapture exploded within her. She cried out wordlessly, capable only of responding to the spasms of sensation that flung her from the foundations of her life into another realm where anguish and ecstasy mingled.

Dimly she was aware of his climax, seconds after hers, dazedly she lay lax and sweat soaked beneath the weight and pressure of his body. It was impossible to move; tiredness so intense that she couldn't even roll over washed over her in waves. After a long time he said something and moved, stretching himself out beside her.

The complacent tone of his voice registered; the words did not. With a sigh, she allowed herself to be turned into his arms and surrendered to sleep.

Morning came in with very little fanfare, a gradual lightening of the darkness, and then the triumphant birth of the sun and the flood of light through the uncurtained windows.

Kathy lay still in the bed; she had woken so slowly that she had been turning over those last words he had spoken for some minutes before she realised she was awake.

'Yes,' he had said. 'I can't see why we shouldn't have a very satisfactory marriage. Sex is certainly not going to be a problem.'

Not for him, perhaps. She winced as she turned over. He was gone, and the bed felt empty and sullied. Muscles she had never known existed ached. If he had said he loved her, she would have smiled with sleepy triumph.

But he did not love her.

He wanted her. Perhaps he felt remorseful at the cruelty of his revenge, and hoped that marriage might make up a little for his betrayal. While she, poor fool, loved him with an all-encompassing emotion.

But he did not love her...

If she married him it would destroy her, it would tear her to bits. She had seen enough of Chris's anguish, loving a woman who desired him but did not love him in return. She was not strong enough to bear such a life, and she was not strong enough to stand against André if he should try to persuade her.

For long minutes, as the day grew around her, she tried to convince herself that she could be happy with him, locked into a loveless marriage. He would be loyal, she knew that. In spite of his somewhat unusual sense of morality he had principles, and he stuck to them. She knew him well enough by now to know that she could expect fidelity, and support, and unswerving courtesy.

Her skin crawled. And she could expect more nights like last night, when the ferocious self-control splintered and he took her into realms of passion and ecstasy that robbed her of any resistance.

It would be unbearable to live with him, bear his children, be a companion and friend and lover, if he did not love her. She discovered greed in herself, a need to know that she came first with him, as he did with her.

For a few futile seconds she tried to persuade herself that he might come to love her. But she was no longer the inexperienced girl who had fallen headlong into love with him. He might come to respect her, even like her, but he would never love her. André didn't believe in love.

She never actually made a decision. She simply couldn't bear to lie any longer in the bed tossed and scented by their lovemaking, so she got up and showered, then left the silent house and walked three miles down the road to a farmhouse from which she called Libby, who arrived within minutes, and took her back down to Auckland.

They had been there no longer than half an hour when the telephone rang. Automatically, because she was the closest, Kathy picked it up.

'Kathy?'

It was André, his voice sharp and angry. Swallowing, she said, 'Yes?'

'I thought as much,' he said savagely. 'I'll be there in half an hour.'

'No.' When he said nothing she went on in a voice she tried to make steady. 'I don't want to see you again.'

'Too bad.' And he hung up.

She stared at Libby, panic making her witless. 'What am I going to do?'

'Well, you can stay and have it out with him or find a refuge until he's calmed down a bit,' Libby said practically, but she too looked hunted.

Desperate, her mind going around in circles, Kathy considered locking herself in and refusing to see him. However, she knew enough of his resourcefulness to understand that he would get his own way somehow.

Her teeth worried her bottom lip. She looked at last year's calendar with her schedule written on it, and read a note addressed to her from Brent.

Brent! With trembling fingers she dialled his number, hoping against hope that he had returned from his family Christmas. It seemed forever until she heard his pleasant voice, and then she almost sobbed with relief.

'What's the matter?' he asked sharply when he recognised her voice. 'You sound sick.'

'No, but could I—Brent, could I stay with you overnight? I wouldn't ask, only I—I need a refuge.'

'Of course you can,' he said instantly. 'I'll come and
get you.'

'Straight away,' she whispered.

'Immediately.'

When she put the receiver down she explained what
was going to happen then suggested, 'You could go back
home, if you wanted to.'

'I'll do that. I don't want to meet André at the
moment, thank you very much. Where is he?'

'Half an hour away.'

'Orewa, probably. I'll go back home through
Helensville and Wellsford, and that way there's no
possibility of our meeting.'

'I—thank you very much.'

Libby gave her a quick hug. 'Look after yourself, love.'

Brent was as good as his word, arriving within ten
minutes and asking no questions until they reached his
flat. Then he took her hands, his own closing tightly
around them. 'What's happened?'

'I—can't tell you.'

'All right,' he said quietly. 'Sit down and I'll make
you a cup of tea.'

Grateful for his uncomplicated loyalty, she smiled. 'I'd
like that. Thank you.'

Brent was essentially kind. She should, she thought
with exhausted gratitude, have fallen in love with him;
it would have made her life much easier.

He brushed aside her stumbling thanks with an airy
rejoinder. 'That's what friends are for, Kathy. And we
are friends, aren't we?'

'Yes, of course,' she said, her voice flat and uninflected. Frowning, she looked at him, her eyes travelling
slowly over his nice craggy face, so honest and open, so

frank and kind. 'I feel as though I'm imposing on you,' she said slowly.

He shrugged. 'You'd do the same for me, wouldn't you?'

She didn't have to think. 'Yes.'

'There you are, then. Now, how about you have a long bath and then get into bed? I've got a couple of lawns to mow and I'll be home about six and if you feel like it you can tell me about it then. If not we'll have dinner and you can go back to bed and when you wake up tomorrow morning things won't seem quite so bad. Trust me, they never do.'

His kind, uncomplicated care was just what she needed. Obediently she allowed him to organise her. She didn't sleep, lying in his comfortable bedroom, numbly reliving the maddened hours of the night before because that was the only way she could stop herself from bursting into tears. Somehow she knew that once the floodgates were opened she would collapse. She had to remain strong.

When he came home she ate as much of the dinner he prepared as she could, and almost immediately went back to bed. He scoffed at her objection to taking the only bed in the flat, saying cheerfully, 'My dear, I have a superlatively comfortable sofa-bed in the sitting-room. I'll sleep on that.'

His bed was large and comfortable. She had brought nothing from André's bach, and in the rush to leave the flat she had forgotten that she needed a nightdress, but she wasn't at all worried about stripping right off and crawling between the sheets. Exhaustion rolled over in wonderful, deadening waves.

Noises woke her from the deep sleep of shock, loud voices and a crash. She bolted upright, her hands grabbing the sheet to pull around her naked form. Brent was yelling, his voice defiant and angry. Then someone

answered in soft, deadly tones, and she went icy cold
with shock and fear. How had André traced her here?

Before she had time to react the door into the bedroom
was thrown open with a crash, the light switched on by
a merciless hand, and he said calmly, 'I don't think I
believe you, Sheridan. She is definitely here, snugly
ensconced in your bed.'

The green glass opacity of his eyes warned her. She
drew in a deep breath, feeling as though she were inhaling
ice crystals, and with a tongue that felt paralysed en-
deavoured to speak. Words didn't come.

'Nothing,' André said thoughtfully, 'could be cosier.'

He was across the room before either could move. One
lean brown hand flicked the sheet back with casual
insolence. 'And naked,' he said, showing his teeth.
'Kathy doesn't sleep naked normally.'

Kathy whispered, 'André, it's not——'

But Brent broke in, his voice oddly loud. 'All right,
now that you've discovered us *in flagrante delicto*, what
do you think you can do?'

'This,' André said. His hand moved, swung, and Brent
received a crashing blow to the jaw. He went down like
a fallen obelisk. André touched his recumbent form
contemptuously with the tip of his toe. His eyes swung
to Kathy, paralysed with horror in the big double bed.
'You didn't need to go to such extremes,' he remarked
conversationally. 'A simple refusal to marry me would
have been enough, you little slut.'

CHAPTER SIX

ON THE first day after the August holidays the school bus arrived back a little early. In fact, Kate was still at her sewing-machine when she heard the toot at the bottom of the hill that signified the descent of her daughter at the end of the narrow, muddy road.

'Rats,' she muttered, hurtling out of the small untidy room she called her office.

Fleur hated not being met, and, being Fleur, didn't hesitate to let her mother know about it. She had a touch of her father's arrogance.

A momentary chill, like an upwelling of fear, tightened the hairs on Kate's skin. Resolutely, as she had done so often in the past six years, she thrust the memory of the man who was Fleur's father to the back of her mind. It was over, and he could no longer hurt her. She had taken back control of her own life, the control she had ceded to him, stupid little fool that she had been, with such a loving, humble, juvenile totality all those years ago.

She had even changed her name. Kathy Townsend no longer existed; she had kept the promise she had made to herself when André said, 'Kathy' with that little hook of contempt in his voice. She was now *Kate* Townsend, an entirely different person.

Hurriedly she strode down the short steep road through the tall trees, taking great lungfuls of the cool, sparkling air, scented with unmistakable, never-forgotten perfume of the New Zealand bush. No time to gaze out over the loveliest view in the world, across the fertile flats and out over the bay, then to the Mercury Islands in the distance that gave this area of the Coromandel peninsula its name of Mercury Bay.

Just before rounding the last corner she heard Fleur's voice, and frowned. Her daughter was the only child to get off the school bus here. Although the road went on for another two miles there was only one other house on it, the homestead at Kaurinui, the rather run down sheep and cattle station that took up most of the hills and several large valleys in the range behind. The Fairchilds, who lived in the homestead and managed the station, were middle-aged and childless.

Still, Fleur didn't sound frightened; not that anything much alarmed the child, but she was laughing, the clear notes ringing confidently out in the crystal air.

Nevertheless, 'Come on,' Kate adjured herself, and began to walk even faster, corduroy-covered legs striding out as she broke from the shade of the trees into the sunlight beyond. The dancing light dazzled her, but she could discern a vehicle, a large opulent Range Rover, and the man leaning on the bumper, teeth flashing in his dark lean face as he laughed with her daughter.

Who was, Kate was glad to see, not too close. She was keeping the lessons so carefully instilled well in mind. As she came up both man and child looked her way and Fleur said cheerfully, 'See, here's Mummy. I told you she'd come to meet me—she always does.'

He straightened, turning towards Kate, the lithe body beneath the olive-green shirt twisting in a tantalising movement that displayed only too well broad shoulders and lean hips above long legs.

Her heart stopped. Shattered, all she could think of was that she must have sensed his aura, for she hadn't remembered him for months until a few minutes ago.

His face hardened, the angles and planes that gave him such potent appeal suddenly stark and uncompromising. The deep green eyes blazed. Then the self-possession that so rarely deserted him came back, and

his features relaxed, settling back into their usual severe
symmetry and the shutters came down over his eyes,
rendering them opaque as he sent her a long unsmiling
look.

'Hello, Kathy,' he said coolly. 'What a long time since
we saw each other last.'

It was only the fact that he was as surprised as she
that gave her enough composure to say quickly, care-
lessly, 'Yes.'

Fleur broke in. 'Do you know Mr Hunter?' she demanded, her astonishment palpable. 'Why does he call
you Kathy? Your name is Kate.'

'A long time ago I was called Kathy,' Kate told her
crisply. An ironic, rather unpleasant smile tugged at the
beautifully moulded mouth of the man she had once
loved with every fibre of her silly tender heart. Ignoring
it, she said, 'When I was young, when I knew Mr Hunter.
We must go home now. Thank Mr Hunter for keeping
you company, Fleur.'

He listened to the child's thanks with a charming air
of interest, making her a slave for life with his smile,
but as they turned to go he suggested, 'I'm going up the
road. Hop in, and I'll give you a lift.'

'No, thank you,' Kate said crisply.

Fleur tugged at her hand. 'Why not, Mummy? My
legs are tired.'

Kate gave her an admonitory smile. 'You are never
tired,' she said sweetly. 'And it's good for you to have
a little walk after being stuck inside all day. Come on.'

Something in the stance of the man by the Range Rover
dragged Kate's eyes his way. He was watching his
daughter, his eyes drifting from Kate's copper-brown
head to Fleur's fiery curls, and his terrible stillness
stopped the heart in her breast. Sickening panic clutched
at her stomach; she took a deep breath, resisting her
first impulse to shield her child, only just managing to
stop herself from stepping protectively in front of her.

Then he looked back up, the green eyes lit from behind by flames in the way she remembered so well. 'So you did marry him after all,' he said almost reflectively.

Woodenly, striving to prevent the strain from showing, she returned, 'No.'

'No?' His lip curled unpleasantly. 'Did you spurn him after one night too? So much for your efforts to convince me that there was nothing between you.'

The old sick terror kicked in her stomach, but this time she refused to give in to it. 'I have never,' she said coldly, 'enjoyed peas porridge nine days old. It's over.'

That whiplike glance flicked back to Fleur, whose small face was wearing an expression of enquiry and budding uneasiness. 'How old are you, sweetheart?' he asked, the caressing note in his voice irresistible.

But Fleur looked at him with some reserve. Acutely intelligent, and wary in the way of small children, she sensed the tension. 'I'm five,' she informed him politely, moving a little closer to the slender upright figure of her mother.

When the quick calculation was computed he looked at Kate with contempt and what appeared to be loathing. 'I wondered, you know,' he said silkily. 'Even when I found you—together—I wondered whether it was just a ploy to get rid of me. You seemed so innocent, so virginal. But that was a lie, too.'

Stirring uneasily, Fleur slipped a warm little hand into Kate's. 'Mummy?' she asked.

Kate tore her eyes away from André's. Reassuringly she smiled, squeezing Fleur's hand. The little girl looked from her to the man who stood tall and dark and as dangerously attractive as an avenging angel, then he too smiled, that special smile that had convinced an eighteen-year-old Kathy that this man, so sophisticated, so stunningly fascinating, loved her. It was just as false now as it had been then, but Fleur was another one not immune to its spell. Slowly she smiled back.

'Mr Hunter and I quarrelled a long time ago, before you were born,' Kate explained briskly, striving to sound unconcerned and ordinary. 'We were young and silly then. Now we're both grown-up we're not going to argue any more, are we, Mr Hunter?'

She fixed him with the same sort of look she had given Fleur, stern, a little chiding, and like Fleur he reacted with a fleeting smile and capitulation. 'No, we're not.' But there was no warmth in the calculating glance that seared her face. 'In fact, Fleur, to show you that we're going to be friends, your mother is going to let me give you a lift home.'

Hoist by her own petard. There was nothing she could do about it, but she made a mental note not to forget that André was like a cat; he had the ability to turn almost every situation to his own advantage. Over the years she had carefully ignored his name in the newspapers but even so she could not avoid the knowledge that in these last six years he had become a very rich, very powerful man.

Wordlessly, her smile set, she surrendered, bustling Fleur into the opulent Range Rover then carefully checking her boots for mud before moving aside André's casual cotton drill driver's jacket, and making sure her seatbelt was done up properly.

'Don't fuss, it's a working vehicle,' he said calmly, shutting the door on her as she attended to her own. After he had swung in beside her he finished, 'How far up the road to you live?'

'About a quarter of a mile.'

He hadn't been up here or he would have known that there was only one other house on the road. Her curiosity had been temporarily dampened by the fearful complex of emotions that battered her when she saw him, but it surfaced again now, raging. However, she wasn't going to ask him what he was doing in this part of the country. In the back Fleur grinned hugely with excitement as the big vehicle moved away from the verge.

He asked with calm deliberation, 'And do you leave your daughter every afternoon at the mercy of anyone who might come along?'

She said with unresponsive blandness, 'No.'

From the back Fleur asked chattily, 'Were you working, Mummy?'

'Yes, darling.'

'Sometimes Mummy forgets,' Fleur confided, 'and she goes on sewing, but not us'ly when it's time for me to come home. Only at night, so the alarm clock has to ring a long time before it wakes her in the morning.'

The cool green gaze slanted sideways. 'Does it? And what work is it that's so fascinating you forget the time?'

Gazing stonily ahead, Kate said, 'I dressmake.'

A short silence. 'Indeed,' he murmured.

Her eyes lingered unwillingly on his hands, long-fingered and lean, their cruel strength apparent even in their grace. She said stonily, 'Yes. And here is our gateway...'

But he drove across the cattle stop and into the tree-shaded courtyard at the side of the house. As she turned to supervise Fleur he said with curt distinctness, 'I'm not going to contaminate either of you.'

Desperate to get away, she jumped down. 'Say thank you to Mr Hunter, sweetheart.'

Fleur chorused her thanks, her expression cautious as she stood beside her mother. Kate knew they looked alike; her daughter had her thin face, wide at the temples, and both had the distinctive cleft chin and golden eyes, although Fleur's had a greenish tinge. Now Kate realised that Fleur had inherited something else from her father; that smooth, supple grace, and the way her brows winged upwards at the outer ends.

Nothing more, thank God.

She gave him a quick meaningless smile. 'Thank you,' she said politely, evenly. 'And goodbye.'

He too smiled, and although there was as little humour in it as there had been in Kate's it was full of significance. 'For the present,' he said as he put the engine into gear.

Her composure snapped. 'What—what do you mean?'

Those winged brows rose. 'Sooner or later it may occur to you to wonder how I happened to be on the road. I'm going to look over Kaurinui to see whether I want to buy it,' he said smoothly. 'I think I'm going to decide in favour. So we'll be neighbours.'

Numbly Kate watched the Range Rover disappear down the short drive, heard the note of the engine change as it began to climb past the house. There was no rattle of stones, no struggling to manoeuvre it around the sharp corner; as in everything he did, André Hunter was more than competent, he excelled.

And that included revenge, she thought starkly.

Fleur had run into the house, leaving her standing on the flagstones. Sudden, terrified tears scorched her face; angrily she dashed them away. She was no longer an inexperienced little girl of eighteen with a head stuffed full of romantic dreams. Now twenty-four, she was a mature women with a career and a child. She had endured much in the past six years, had to call on all her resources to come through it all, and if she wasn't exactly triumphant—well, there were victories where triumph had no place.

It was a good life she had made for her daughter and herself, one that was satisfying and worthwhile, and she was not going to let a ghost from the past destroy it. Even though he might soon own her house. He didn't yet realise that her cottage stood on Kaurinui land.

For a moment the sick fear she had felt too often in her life rose to block her throat, but she fought it back.

Time enough to worry about finding a new place to live in if he threw her out.

'Mummy, can I have a norange?'

'May I have,' she corrected automatically, turning away from the sparkling day and going into the small house that was her refuge and her home. 'Yes, but I'll peel it for you.'

When her daughter was seated at the table with a glass of milk and the orange, Kate went swiftly into the office and put the exquisite silk dress she was working on away. Until Fleur went to bed work was over for the day.

But she stood for a long moment, her eyes sightlessly staring at the steep forested hills that separated her from the homestead at Kaurinui, as the past crawled up out of the limbo to which she had assigned it. Although the room was warm, she shivered.

She had thought she had left it all behind; she should have known that New Zealand, with its tiny population, had no place to hide.

Later that evening, when her daughter was in bed and the laughter and fun had faded into a silence only broken by the soft hiss of the flames, she sat down in front of the old tiled fireplace and gazed around the room. She had moved here just after Fleur had been born. Mr Fairchild had at first refused to rent it because it had been in such a bad condition, but he had relented when she had begged. Looking back, she thought he had probably seen the panic in her eyes.

He had been kind. But then, they were all kind; he and his wife had cleaned up the house before she moved in, and he had somehow managed to wring money from his notoriously stingy employers to mend the plumbing and the electricity. Beth Beatson, the wife of the farmer down the road, had arrived the day Kate moved in, with a large meat pie and a plate of scones, and stayed to become the first of her friends here. There had been plenty of others made since then, but Beth was still her dearest one. Was it five years ago?

Her soft mouth, disciplined in a hard school, trembled. Heartsick and bitter when she found herself pregnant and betrayed, she had been positive that she had nothing to offer anyone. Until she had looked into the face of her newborn daughter and fallen in love, more surely, more sanely than she had with the baby's father.

For of course she had never really loved André. How could she have? She had been such a child. Her sheltered life had left her unskilled in the art of dealing with the masculine half of humanity. When André, with his striking good looks and aura of sensual expertise, had stalked her, she had taken one look at him from her golden eyes and fallen in love, copper head over slender heels.

A puff of gas ignited in the manuka log in the fire, sending a blue flame upwards. Sighing, she got up to put on the kettle in the kitchen.

Once back in the sitting-room she turned the lights off and sat quietly sipping tea. At eighteen she had been ripe for love, aching to taste the fruits of knowledge. Her sensuality had been blossoming, her awareness of her attraction to men building, and with it all had come a certain dangerous preening pride in her femininity.

The car accident had unbalanced her, especially the brutal aftermath, rendering her both vulnerable and in need of consolation. And with Chris locked in the prison of his own pain and unable to help, she had had no one to turn to. If André hadn't hunted her down, harbouring black revenge in his heart, there would probably have been another man, and that was her bad luck. Another man might have let her down a little more lightly.

Unbidden, her mind recalled André as he had been that afternoon. He too had changed. His ruthlessness had been transmuted into a chilling purposefulness, more dangerous because it was more directed, backed up with an unflinching authority that had not been so blazingly obvious then.

She moved uneasily, avoiding her own personal knowledge of just how relentless he could be. Thank heavens he had seen nothing of himself in Fleur. It was unlikely that he ever would. Apart from that elusive grace, André's daughter did not resemble him openly.

But he had the right to know that he had a daughter. And Fleur, Kate thought with a sigh, had also the right to know her father.

As always when she thought of this, a cold, sick anger tasted foul in her mouth. If he knew that he had a daughter, how would he react? Would he ignore her, or worse, would he want her?

Kate's heart thudded shallowly in her breast. Would he demand access to his daughter?

Shivering, she recalled the contemptuous glance he had given her when he had realised how old Fleur was. Of course, he could always refuse to believe that she was his daughter!

That, she thought with a smile that managed to combine wryness with worry, might be the very best thing that could happen. Unfortunately, she didn't believe it would. He was not stupid, and he would know that there was some chance of her being his child. Neither of them had used any protection that night. And he was possessive enough to want access to his daughter.

Restlessly she picked up her cup and took it into the kitchen, washed it, and made Fleur's lunch for the next day, wrapping it in plastic film. The wind pounced on to the house, snatched at a window. From the front room came a creak, the comforting sound of an old house settling down for the night.

She glanced at the clock. Eight o'clock. Three hours until bedtime. Normally she would work, but this prickly unease kept her away from the machine, and for once she wasn't sewing to a deadline so her conscience was clear.

The telephone chirruped into the silence. Frowning, she picked up the receiver. 'Hello.'

Beth Beatson said cheerfully, 'Goodness, what an apprehensive voice! All well?'

Relaxing, the tight, strained note easing into her normal husky tones, she said, 'Yes, of course. How are you?'

'Oh, as usual. A stone overweight and very much overworked, but I'll get there. How would you like to come to a barbecue tomorrow night?'

'A barbecue?' Outside the rain drummed mercilessly on the roof. 'Living dangerously, aren't you?'

Beth chuckled. 'Yep, but we'll have it in the woolshed. Simon'll spit-roast a weaner pig and we can dance afterwards if we want to.'

'What are you celebrating?'

'We got an excellent price for our bulls at the sale, and we thought we'd like to have a small fling.'

'Sounds a great idea.' Like most cattle and sheep farmers the Beatsons had had a bad few years so if they wanted to celebrate the turning of the tide Kate was more than happy to help.

'Right, bring Fleur and we'll pop her into bed with Emma. The boys are going to watch videos until we call it a day. Or a night, I suppose.'

The two Beatson boys, Fergus and Sean, were at high school and so had another week of holidays. They were nice responsible lads, and Kate knew they could be relied upon to keep an eye on the girls. Anyway, she thought, she wouldn't stay too late.

As she hung up, having suggested that she bring a pavlova and a salad—suggestions which were eagerly accepted by Beth—she was smiling, the fears and shock held temporarily at bay. This, she thought, was her life now; it was serene and eminently satisfying, although

Beth would no doubt have an unmarried man there to introduce to her. Beth was happily married herself, and her matchmaking had become a joke between them, but laugh as Beth did at herself she didn't give up, saying that Kate needed a good man for support and fun. Unfortunately the last thing Kate wanted to do was risk her hard-won peace on the throw of a dice! Still, at least Beth was never obvious about it.

When she dreamed that night it was of the night of Fleur's conception. Her memories had faded by the time she woke up but she spent that day fighting a feeling of sad forlornness that intensified as she put on a swirl of skirt in heavy rust cotton, teaming it with a forest-green shirt and jacket, separated by a woollen waistcoat in a lighter shade of the skirt colour. Beneath it she wore green socks and Doc Marten shoes; perhaps not the sort of clothes one would expect a sober mother to wear, she thought as she eyed herself in the mirror, but in a way she was advertising her prowess as a dressmaker, and there was no doubt that the outfit suited her to perfection and was entirely suitable for a woolshed barbecue and dancing afterwards.

'Hurry up, Mummy.' Fleur wriggled down from the bed, her vibrant little body clad in jeans and a heavy jersey in the clear corn-yellow that suited her so well, and incidentally made her easy to pick out in a throng. 'Emma says Sean and Fergus are going to watch a horror movie and I want to see it too.'

'I doubt very much whether they are,' her mother said drily. 'And you, my darling, are going to be in bed before they watch any movies.'

Fleur wailed, 'But, Mummy——'

'The boys don't have to go to school tomorrow; the high school gets an extra week, as you well know.'

'It's not fair!'

'Tell me that when you reach high school, and I'll
listen. But rest assured, there will be no videos for you
tonight.'

Fleur sighed ostentatiously but she was a sunny-
tempered child, soon over her small flares of temper,
and when they left the house in the old car Kate just
managed to afford she was singing and happy again,
looking forward to the party with an intensity that
sometimes alarmed her mother.

It had to be another legacy from her father. Kate
couldn't remember feeling things with such ferocity; she
had been a placid child. Whereas André, although he
managed to hide them behind the mask of self-
containment, suffered from fierce emotions. Witness his
decision to punish her for her part in Olivia's death.

And, she thought, suddenly remembering her dreams
of the night before, his savage tenderness when they had
made love. For the first time in years she blushed, cursing
beneath her breath the man who had come back into
her life with such devastating effect.

Had he bought Kaurinui? Oh, how she hoped it was
not what he wanted! Still, it would be time to worry
about that when she knew one way or the other, she
decided, turning off the road.

The Beatsons' yard was filled with cars and Land
Rovers, and the woolshed was irradiated with light. At
first glance it seemed that Beth had invited almost
everyone from the district, and a few who were not. As
she took in her contributions to the meal Kate was greeted
with cheerful amiability on all sides. Giving as good as
she got, she glowed, realising again how lucky she was
to have found a district where the fact that she was an
unmarried mother seemed not to matter a whit.

She had found her niche, and she was not going to
let André Hunter's arrival on the scene put her off it.

'Oh, you do superb pavs!' Beth swooped on it with
rapturous cries. 'Look at that, and so beautifully dec-

orated with kiwi fruit slices! I think kiwi fruit and pavs
were designed to go together. Bless you, Kate, just put
them down here and then come and meet the few people
you don't know. Come on, Fleur, Emma's over by the
barbecue. She says she's helping her daddy, but *I* think
she's working out which are going to be the best bits of
crackling, greedy little minx.'

Fleur giggled and darted off ahead to a wide space
where the barbecue had been set up. Already the number
of people had warmed the somewhat chilly atmosphere,
and the noise and laughter were of a level to warm any
anxious hostess's heart. It was clearly going to be a good
evening.

'Here we are, and here is André Hunter, who has just
signed up for Kaurinui,' Beth said with a significant
glance at the woman beside her. 'André, this is——'

'But we know each other,' André said smoothly, green
eyes gleaming with mockery. Before Kate had a chance
to say anything, he took her hand and lifted it to his
mouth. 'We met—oh, six years ago, wasn't it, Kate? And
yesterday afternoon Fleur introduced us all over again.'

His mouth was warm and sensuous, and to her horror
she felt a savage pang of need streak along her nerve-
ends. Dimly she was aware of Beth's laughter and ex-
clamations; dimly she realised that Fleur was holding up
her pert little face for a kiss; in misery so extreme she
thought she might die of it she saw him lift her daughter's
little paw and, with a grace that had to come from his
Latin ancestors, kiss it too. Fleur beamed, her eyes
sparkling with mingled delight and mischief, then allowed herself to be taken off by Emma to admire the
pig on the spit.

Beth's stare was curiosity unbounded, but she man-
fully struggled to hide it and said smartly, 'Super! New
Zealand is so small, isn't it? Look, excuse me while I
go and look after the Carpenters, will you? They've just
arrived and they're both rather shy. André, can I ask

you to get Kate a drink? The bar is over there by the shearing platform.'

The almost unseemly rapidity of her departure left a hole behind, a hole Kate thought she might fall into and be swallowed up by. Nervously she sent him a flickering glance, but as there was nothing to be learned from his enigmatic expression she said quickly, 'You don't need to——'

'Of course I do,' he said softly, smiling at her with such charm that only someone as close as she was, and looking directly at him, would notice how very cold his eyes were. 'You heard our hostess. What will you have to drink?'

'Gin and tonic,' she said, adding quickly, 'I'll wait here.'

He smiled down at her. 'No, I think you should come with me, otherwise I might lose you, and in this crush I could well not find you again.'

She opened her mouth to object, only to subside under the sardonic amusement she saw in his face. She did, however, resist when he took her hand in his, but short of making a full-scale scene there was little she could do to disentangle herself from his warm, uncompromising grip.

'Sensible,' he said softly in her ear. 'We're already the cynosure of all eyes as it is. Is there anyone whose toes I'll be treading on?'

Her teeth bit into her bottom lip. She flashed him a resentful glance and met relentless determination head on. 'No,' she said angrily.

'But what a boring life for you. Or is being a mother enough emotional outlet for you? Somehow, I think not. The Kathy I knew needed much more than the spiritual joys of maternity to keep her warm at night.'

'Shut up,' she hissed, flushing.

His laughter was soft and ironic. 'Yes, you're right, this is hardly the occasion to talk over old times.'

'I don't want to talk over old times,' she snapped, goaded into fury.

'Oh, I think we should. You left such a lot of unfinished business behind you when you ran away. I've always promised myself that if we met again I'd finish it.'

The words were delivered in a perfectly easy tone, but there was a thread of steel through them that warned her she would not enjoy the finishing he spoke of.

Between her teeth she insisted, 'We have nothing to say to each other——'

'Not here, and not now,' he agreed, maddeningly reasonable. 'Ah, here we are at the bar.'

She got her gin and tonic, and he the beer which was apparently all that he was drinking, but in spite of the interest they were arousing she had no chance to escape. He stayed with her all through the evening, refusing to leave her when she introduced other people to him, smiling down at her with a lazy charm that didn't hide the single-minded intensity behind it.

Hatefully aware of the smiles and significant looks being exchanged around them, she tried low-voiced expostulations and direct orders to leave her alone, to no avail. Only she saw the cold detachment at the back of his seeming interest in her, and as the evening wore on she became more afraid than angry.

There were subtle differences between the man she had known and this André. He had always seemed hard to her but this man's will had been tempered by the years into a steely inflexibility. Behind the cool assurance there was now an implacable harshness. The wicked charm and knowing eyes were the same but instead of the easy sang-froid of which she had always been so envious this man was totally self-sufficient; the rockbound confidence showed through.

Only the crackling aura of danger was the same, at once part of the attraction and the best reason for not surrendering to it.

Several times she checked on Fleur, who was having a marvellous time with Emma and several other children there, mostly pretending to help with the barbecue. Her high-spirited laughter rose regularly above the adult chatter and gossip.

'She seems very responsible,' André said, noticing her glance over her shoulder.

'She is, but she's not very old.'

'Has her lack of a father ever bothered her?'

She went a little pale. For once they were alone but even so she looked around a little guiltily. 'No. I—explained, and she's never said anything about it again.'

'Which does not necessarily mean she doesn't think about it.'

She reacted to the hint of censure in the deep voice with an angry flare. 'I know, you don't have to tell me that. So far it doesn't seem to have mattered too much to her. There are other children in the school from broken marriages so she's not alone in only having one parent. And it is none of your business.'

The last bitter observation was promoted by her fear that he might be wondering whether he was Fleur's father.

'I know,' he said bitingly. 'But the child is not to blame for having a slut for a mother.'

Her sharp breath and white face revealed only too clearly how sharply the insult stung. Without saying a word she turned and pushed away from him, her eyes muddied and dark with torment and pain.

'What's the matter?' It was Beth, her laughing face concerned.

Kate drew a deep breath, but it was impossible to tell Beth what had caused her anguish. She managed to smile, shaking her head. 'It's all right. André and I have always quarrelled, and this is just another one.'

Beth's gaze sharpened, but she said merely, 'What a pity, because he's gorgeous, isn't he? And Mr Fairchild has been singing his praises to Simon all evening. Apparently he's going to do great things at Kaurinui. He must be really rich.'

Kate answered the question behind the observation with a pale smile. 'Yes. Excessively so.'

'Just as well, because the place needs an awful lot of ready money spent on it to bring it up to production. Joe Cameron's widow wouldn't spend a cent on the place—she drained it dry. I'm glad someone is going to look after it again.' She looked beyond Kate again. 'I suppose if you look like him and have money too you tend to get a bit spoiled. Although he doesn't seem that way. Too—too tough behind that stunning charm.'

'Yes, he's tough,' Kate said remotely. 'Mr Fairchild will be earning his pay.'

'Are you all right?'

She gave her friend a swift glittering smile, hiding as best she could the anger smouldering beneath it. It made her feel ill, yet for the first time in years she was fully alive, brain working furiously, reacting to the quick-silver surge of emotions she had struggled to suppress over the last few years.

'Yes, I'm fine,' she said mendaciously, because this eagerness, this wildfire anticipation, was what had got her into so much trouble when she was eighteen. She didn't want to have to cope with those wayward un-inhibited responses once more. She was not going to have her control ripped away to reveal the sensitive woman behind the practicality.

'Ah,' Beth said, after another shrewd look. 'Simon's giving me the sign. The pork must be ready.'

'I'll help you with the supper.'

Beth accepted the offer with alacrity, organising her and the other women who gravitated to the two large tables that had been set out behind the shearing stalls. Unfortunately, one of them was unable to contain herself and asked about André, her curiosity for the most part kindly, but galling for all that.

'We met when I lived in Auckland.' Yes, that was the right note, serene, almost amused. 'But I haven't seen or heard anything of him for—oh, it must be six or seven years now.'

'He's bought Kaurinui, I heard.'

She pinned a smile to her face. 'So Beth said.'

'I don't know why he'd want to buy such a rundown place, it's going to be years before he gets a return on his investment. Still, he looks like a man who knows what he's doing, and what he wants.' She finished with an arch smile.

Kate could feel her cheeks burning like hot coals, but even as she grimly told herself that Mary Service was a kindly woman, if inclined to gossip too much, her eyes found the place where André stood talking to the wife of one of the farmers.

As though she had sent him a signal across the woolshed he turned, and for a second they stared each other down, grave, unsmiling, while the air danced and crackled between them. Shaken, she dragged her eyes free and helped set out the food.

Supper was delicious, the smooth sweet pork tenderly grilled, set off to perfection by winter salads and the jacket-roasted potatoes that had been cooking in the embers. Afterwards Kate decided in the most cowardly manner to slip away home, but when she looked at her daughter, her eager little face suffused with pleasure at the prospect of going to bed in Emma's room, she knew that she couldn't do it. However, she went across to the house with the girls and got them washed and tucked up, spinning out the process until she could no longer put off going back to the woolshed.

Looking in on the boys in the sitting-room, engaged in winning World War Two all over again, she said, 'I'm off. If they haven't settled down in half an hour, threaten them with a mother, will you?'

'Yes,' Sean and Fergus said absently.

'Goodnight.'

With a rueful shake of her head she went back through the chilly damp night, back to the woolshed and the music that was emanating from it.

And of course there was André, leaning against the wall by the door, smiling at a small circle about him with the unforced charm that was so lethally potent. Without seeming to look her way he straightened up as she came in, said something that set both men and women laughing, and caught her up before she had taken four steps.

'Dance with me,' he said softly.

She shook her head. 'I don't dance.'

'Why? Do you give too much away when you dance?'

The floor by the woolpress was smooth and shiny, and the music came from an old-time dance band that played around the district mostly for their own enjoyment. Her shoulders moved uneasily. 'I haven't danced in years,' she said stubbornly, refusing to acknowledge his question. 'Anyway, I can't do these old-fashioned dances.'

The leader of the band put down his beer and called for gentlemen to take their partners for a Valeta. No concessions to feminism here, she thought, looking around for an escape route.

'I'll show you.'

Startled, she looked up, and drowned in the gleaming jungle of his eyes. 'I grew up in the country,' he said, his narrow smile sharp as a knife. 'I spent my adolescence being initiated into the mysteries of Military Twosteps and the Maxina.'

His hand on her waist wouldn't be denied; he swept her on to the floor and that was that. He moved fluidly, with a lithe masculine grace, that was completely familiar yet threatening. She knew that their steps matched. She knew that when they moved together it was as one person, perfectly matched, caught up by a sense of rhythm that flowed between them in an irresistible force.

His arm across her back was firm, his hand around hers warm, even secure, as he guided her through the steps. After several minutes of concentration she found them coming easily, but that gave her no pleasure, for without the concentration to keep her mind busy it was free to wander to other things, like the faint male fragrance of him, a classic, potently subliminal aura that set her senses spinning.

And the feel of his body, lean-muscled and taut against her. He didn't hold her too tight, but she was close enough to feel the flexion and play of muscles as he moved, and recognise her own helpless, hateful response.

CHAPTER SEVEN

KATE woke the next morning to confusion and anger, and at the bottom a deep despair, because that dance, the only one they had shared, told her how utterly flimsy were her hopes of keeping André at a distance. The attraction between them was as strong as it had ever been.

Making her excuses as soon as she could, she had picked up Fleur and fled to the sanctuary of her home to lie awake for half the night, her brain going round and round in circles as she wondered whether she should run again, knowing that it was already too late. As fast and as far as she could run, the world held no place to hide from her emotions.

The next day he rang just after Fleur had gone to bed, his dark male voice falling into her silence. 'Hello. I didn't realise that your cottage is on Kaurinui. I'll take you out tomorrow night to discuss things. Be ready at seven o'clock.'

'No, I can't——'

His voice hardened, yet paradoxically became softer. 'Of course you can. After all, you owe me.'

'Owe——?' But he had hung up. Kate listened with incredulous anger to the silence, then took the receiver away from her ear and stared at it, before crashing it back into place.

'I am not going out with you,' she said grimly into the silent air, then flounced into her sewing-room, closing the door behind her with a small thud.

She sewed with grim concentration until bedtime, glad that she had trained herself to work no matter what the turmoil in her life.

But when she was in her bed, listening to the wind rise outside, she couldn't settle, her mind going over and over again the summer they had met, the ecstasy, the precarious happiness, and the crushing grief at his betrayal. And the long, sweet, tumultuous hours of that last night, when he had tenderly, rapturously, taught her all that she knew about making love. It was a bitter pill to realise that André still had the power to set her alight with one glance.

Of course now she knew that it wasn't love. Overwhelming attraction, lust, carnality—it had many names, love had only one. She wanted André. Physically they were attuned. It was as easy—and as difficult—as that. Which was no doubt why he wanted to take her out to dinner the following night. Her lip curled. An opportunist to the end.

When at last she drifted off to sleep it was with an ironclad determination not to give in, not to surrender again to that unholy desire. Perhaps there had been some excuse for her whole-hearted submersion in the waters of passion at eighteen. She had been a child in experience and knowledge. Now she was a mature mother, intelligent and sensible enough to make sure that she never gave it the chance to happen again.

And, she thought, her last thought before unconsciousness claimed her, she wasn't going out with him, either. If he came looking for her tomorrow night it would be to discover Fleur tucked in bed and no babysitter.

But of course she knew he'd come. As seven o'clock approached she found herself looking anxiously towards the clock; in spite of a very vigorous mental chiding she had put on an elegant pair of saffron trousers, pleated and full, vaguely harem-like in cut, topping them with a paprika camisole and a silk shirt the same colour as the trousers. He would know damned well that she didn't normally wear clothes like that for a quiet night at home, she thought grimly, but if he wanted to stay he could join her in eating the very hearty beef casserole that was simmering richly in the oven. She had no intention of putting her peaceful, satisfactory life in jeopardy by going out with him.

Sure enough, the lights of a car prowled up the drive at five to seven; she tensed, her hands suddenly lacing painfully together. Would it have been better to acquiesce to his high-handed demand? Defiance was hardly tactful. A sudden downpour made her jump; there should be lightning, she thought fancifully, waiting for the knock with a kind of smouldering resignation.

But when it came she opened the door to him with a calm assurance that might have intimidated a less confident man.

André, however, allowed himself a long, cool survey of her slender body in the orientally coloured outfit, then smiled. 'Like something out of the Arabian nights,' he drawled. 'Beautiful and passionate and different. Aren't you going to invite me in?'

'Only if you accept that I'm not going out with you tonight.'

His eyebrows lifted. 'Only if you invite me to share whatever it is that smells so good.'

It had been what she planned. Here, after all, she would be the one at home, relaxed and confident. But she hesitated, warned by the gleam in his eyes that he had read something else into her invitation.

'Only if you realise that I'm not on the menu,' she returned evenly.

Which gave him another excuse to scan her body. 'Pity,' he drawled. 'You look like the ingredients for an exceptionally delicious curry. However, I'll accept your conditions. Now may I come in? It's freezing out here.'

Wet, too. Firmly banishing a ridiculous urge to flick away the raindrops that sprinkled across his darkly gleaming hair, she opened the door wide. For a moment, as he stepped over the lintel, she was visited by a premonition so acute that she almost cried out with the warning. Goose-pimples started out all over her body; stepping hastily away, she repressed a shiver.

'I like it,' he said after a keen look around the sitting-room.

She drew a deep calming breath. 'Thank you.'

He transferred his glance to her still face, remote with the effort to appear wholly at ease. 'Fairchild told me that it was a mess when you first took it over, and that you've put a lot of work into it.'

'He helped me, and it was structurally sound. I lived in it for a year or so until I'd worked out what I wanted to do.'

Firelight flickered on the painted walls, on the old pressed tin ceiling with its patterns of leaves and flowers, painted white. Bookshelves she had made herself from pine planks rose almost to the ceiling on either side of the fireplace, the array of books lightened by flowers and plants, old carefully framed prints and several pieces of good pottery.

An old pine wardrobe stood in one corner, and in front of the fire were two comfortable wicker sofas that she had discovered in a farmer's barn and painstakingly repaired and repainted. She had also made the blue cushions and piped them in white. A vase held a branch of japonica blossom, its coral flowers opening in the warmth. There were more pictures on the walls, mostly prints she had found and framed herself, and from the mantelpiece beamed a photograph of Fleur. André's eyes rested for a buzzing moment on the vivid little face, but he said nothing.

'Yes, I like it,' he announced slowly. 'Were you re-compensed for the money you spent?'

She said evenly. 'No. Mrs Cameron doesn't like spending money on the station, let alone a worker's cottage. It cost very little. And until I built up the business I had a fair amount of time on my hands.'

Another shower hit the corrugated-iron roof, rattling across it with gusto before settling down to a steady thrum. 'In weather like this, I imagine you had plenty of time.'

She reacted swiftly to the taunt, defending her chosen home with spirit. 'We usually have good weather—very little of Auckland's beastly humidity. Sit down, André. Can I get you a drink?' She gestured at the butler's tray against the wall.

'No, I'll get you one. What do you drink now?'

'There's a half-bottle of Hawke's Bay Sauvignon Blanc there.'

'I'll have a whisky,' he said, and calmly poured out the drinks. 'There. Now, what should we drink to?'

She set her glass down, smiling a little ironically at the amused mockery in his question. 'How about a better day tomorrow?' she suggested.

'For whom? You or me?'

'I didn't think one was exclusive of the other. Are we still enemies, André?'

His lids came down over the crystalline green eyes, hiding his thoughts. It was an effective trick, and one she remembered of old. 'I don't know. Are we?'

'I don't think I was ever your enemy.'

His broad shoulders moved in what could have been an infinitesimal shrug. 'No? I find it hard to believe that you climbed into Brent Sheridan's bed as a friendly gesture.'

Tell him, her mind urged her tongue. Tell him *now*!

If he hadn't been looking at her with such an impassive face, one revealing no kindness nor compassion nor any hint of understanding, she might have. But all she could think of was Fleur, confused by a legal battle over her future.

In a voice she strove to keep objective she said, 'I hadn't slept with him when you came thundering on his door.'

He lifted his lashes and looked straight at her, making no attempt to hide the lashing contempt. 'I prefer it when you tell the truth,' he said scathingly. 'I know what I saw that night.'

She met his gaze with steady intensity, anger turning her eyes to glowing golden jewels. 'What you saw was a girl who was completely at the end of her tether,' she told him without emotion. 'I was running——'

'Yes, straight into bloody Sheridan's arms. He must have thought all his birthdays had come at once,' he interrupted savagely. 'You knew he wanted you. God, when you fronted up I'll bet he couldn't wait to hurry you into his bed.'

'It wasn't like that at all!' Forgetting her resolution to be calm and controlled, she spoke sharply, her cheeks flushing with anger. He had no right to speak of Brent with such scornful contempt.

'Then tell me what it was like. His daughter had to be conceived within a month of your leaving me. Did you hate what we did so much that you wanted to overlay the memories with other, better ones?'

At her gasp he pressed home, the words harsh with distaste. 'Or did you discover a liking for it, so that you couldn't do without it? God knows, you had enough natural talent.'

She clamped down on the surge of righteous anger, her teeth gleaming white in the firelight. Her soft mouth was a thin line, the dimple beside it gone. 'All you need to know,' she said icily, 'all that's relevant to this hypocritical tirade, was that when you came down to Auckland breathing fire and threats I hadn't slept with him.'

He looked at her with a smile that held no amusement, nothing but a vast cynicism. 'If you say so,' he drawled.

'Now, shall we speak about something less contentious? Drink some of your wine and tell me how you happened to end up here, sewing for a living. I know you always had a hankering to live on the Coromandel, but *sewing*?'

The wine was splendid on her tongue, a superb white of taste and flavour. With deliberate care she drank it slowly, enjoying it, until she had regained her composure. 'I always was good at sewing,' she said calmly. 'My mother saw to that. When I came here it seemed the logical thing to do.'

'I see.' He looked into the amber liquid in his glass, tipping it slightly to catch the light. 'I know you didn't get on with your parents, but why didn't you go home when you found yourself pregnant?'

Her mouth twisted. 'I did. But my parents wanted me to have the baby adopted. And I couldn't. So when I had her I came up here.'

'I remember the day we went out on the harbour, that first day I took you out, you said you'd like to go to the Coromandel.'

She sent him a swift, startled look, met his hard, speculative gaze. 'Yes, well, I've never regretted it,' she muttered.

'Did you think of earning your living by sewing then?'

She moved her shoulders a little uneasily and drank some more of the wine. 'No, I was on the benefit. Beth Beatson, my neighbour down the road, was complaining one day because she didn't have a dress to wear to a party, so I offered to make her one. It just grew from there. After about a year I was earning enough to be able to go off the benefit.'

'And do you regret not finishing your degree?'

An ironic smile pulled her soft mouth into a disciplined line. 'Yes, in many ways I do, but when Fleur is older I'll finish it extramurally.'

There was a little silence. Abstracted, his expression unreadable, he watched the flames flare and flow together in the fireplace. Then he began to talk about the current political system.

She relaxed, recalling with wry acknowledgement that he had always been an excellent companion, even in those dreadful days spent at the bach. Amusing and intelligent, with a subtle brain that picked up quickly on the things she left unsaid, he soon had her laughing. Surprised, she caught him watching her, his narrowed eyes gleaming with what seemed perilously like complacence.

Warning bells shrilled in her brain. She had been fooled by this man before, and suffered more than she ever intended to suffer again.

'I'll go and see to dinner,' she muttered, scrambling to her feet.

Once in the kitchen she drew a deep breath and drank some cold water, telling herself sternly that although she shouldn't over-react it would be easy to forget that André was a consummate actor.

The casserole was as resplendent as red wine and herbs and good beef could make it. She lifted it out of the oven and set it to one side of the stove before taking the soup from the element and ladling it into a tureen. The home-made bread was already warm; she carried it through to the table in the dining area, then went through to the sitting-room. André was standing in front of the bookcase looking at the contents, his lean form elegantly disposed, one hand outstretched, the dark, strong fingers curled negligently around the cover of one of her books.

Kate's heart did a strange flip-flop, then settled down again. 'Dinner's ready,' she said briskly.

Book in hand, he swung around. 'It smells superb.'

'Thank you.'

His smile was a taunt. 'But you always were an excellent cook.'

'My mother still believes that a woman's worth is measured solely by how good a housekeeper she is,' she retorted smartly. 'I didn't believe it before and I still don't, but at least she made sure I could do what was necessary in a house. Come and eat.'

It gave her a strange uneasy feeling, half alarm, half guilty pleasure, to be eating with him on opposite sides of the old kauri table. Part of it, she decided, was just the pleasure of seeing someone—anyone—enjoy food she had cooked. It was akin to her delight when the clothes she had made looked good on their owners, the pleasure of an artist in her creation.

But the other part, the part that roused her alarm, was the companionable enjoyment of having a man sit opposite her, the occasional meeting of eyes, the sensual pleasure of being with a magnificent male animal.

And therein, she admitted, lay the danger he represented to her.

When at last the dinner was over she put coffee on to a tray and carried it into the sitting-room. André was stooped, feeding a large log into the fireplace, his hands deft and quick. He stood up as she came in and dusted his hands, watching as she put the tray down on to the table between the sofas.

'Still black?' she asked pleasantly.

He came to sit beside her. 'Yes, thank you.'

It took an effort to pour without her hands trembling but she did it, and then poured her own, adding milk to the dark brew. 'Would you like something to drink?' she suggested. 'At least, it will have to be brandy, as that's all I've got.'

'No, nothing, thank you.' He leaned back, his glittering green glance not leaving her profile.

Mistrusting the intensity of his regard, she hurried into speech. 'Why did you decide to buy Kaurinui?'

He shrugged, a strange little smile pulling at his mouth. 'Land is always an excellent investment.'

'I thought your main interests were urban.'

'No—where we lived in Gisborne was close to the hills, so I grew up with an interest in farming.'

'But here?' she persisted. 'Land in the Coromandel, even the best of it, is marginal, isn't it? There must be much better farms for sale around the country.'

'Perhaps. None so wild, though, so in need of care and attention.'

Yes, once, on the same day she had told him she wanted to go to the Coromandel, he had spoken of the Caird man who had left his lovely island to bring in some neglected land on the mainland; she had noticed and been surprised by the envy in his tone. 'Is Mr Fairchild staying on?'

'Yes. He knows the place like the back of his hand, and he loves it. He needs help, though. I'll put an extra couple of houses on to the place and he can have as many hands as he can keep busy.'

She nodded, nervously dampening dry lips. 'And what about this house?'

'What about it?'

But she wasn't prepared to be tormented. Baldly she said, 'I want to know what you plan to do with it.'

'Nothing,' he said softly, watching her from beneath his drooping eyelids. 'I think everything is very satisfactory as it is now, don't you? Or did you think I was going to throw you out into the rain, Kath—Kate?'

'No.' But she couldn't look him straight in the eyes. 'And you? Will you be spending time here too?'

'Do you want me to?' His voice was soft and infinitely teasing, yet beneath the smooth banter she sensed a hardness.

'I doubt if what I want will have any effect on you,' she returned with a rather desperate composure, 'but it won't make any difference to me. I don't suppose we'll meet much.'

He laughed. 'Perhaps not.' A little silence, and then he asked idly, 'Why didn't you marry Sheridan?'

She bit her lip but common sense overrode the swift defensiveness. 'I—it wasn't—I didn't want to.'

He said quietly, 'I've wondered whether I scarred you too badly by raping you.'

Her head jerked. She saw the familiar mockery, but knew now that it served as a mask for darker, more complex emotions. 'You didn't rape me,' she said curtly. 'I was more than willing.'

'So willing that you ran away, and hopped into Sheridan's bed the next night.' His voice was cool, almost judicial.

If she convinced him that she hadn't he would know that Fleur was his. She sent him a troubled look, veiling her eyes swiftly as they met the rapier probe of his. Holding her breath, she reiterated quietly, 'I hadn't slept with him when you tracked me down.'

'So you say.' He settled back into the sofa, broad shoulders moving a little, the grace he shared with Fleur as potent as ever.

'I don't really see what use it is rehashing the past.' She drank a little of her coffee and set the cup down, mildly pleased at the steadiness of her hand. 'It's over.'

'The past is never done with—its shadow falls over both the present and the future. For example, you won't go out with me because of the past. If we had just met for the first time we would be more than interested.' Beneath the long lashes his eyes were narrowed slivers of green. 'Because it's still there, Kathy.'

'Kate,' she corrected automatically.

'Kate. Yes, I like it, it suits you now, as Kathy did then. But Kate or Kathy, your eyes still show the same startled recognition as they did when you looked up at me in that room in Auckland six years ago.'

'I know now what that is,' she said evenly. 'Lust. It strikes like lightning and, like it, leaves ashes and rubble and destruction behind. I don't want anything to do with it.'

His smile was almost tender, yet there was anticipation and a wolfish enjoyment. 'I can see that. I'm
sorry you were burned, Kate. I was, too. But this isn't
like lightning, which never strikes twice in the same spot.
This is more like a volcano, always there, seething up
from the bowels of the earth, irresistible, all-consuming,
more powerful than any other force of nature.'

'Volcanoes die,' she parried smartly. 'Those hills that
make up the Coromandel peninsula were once torn from
the belly of the earth, but there's no fire there now.'

'Let's see, shall we?' He caught her chin before she
had time to flinch away, and smiled into her dilated eyes.
'Just a little experiment,' he murmured as his mouth
came down on hers.

It was quick, brutally snatched, and she resisted,
holding her mouth still and closed, but she felt the
seething fires of attraction in him and the response deep
within her own traitorous body.

And when it was over, her lips crushed and throbbing,
he looked down at her with laughing scornful eyes and
said, 'Like kissing a flower; beautiful but ultimately
unsatisfactory.'

Her eyes spat sparks at him, and he smiled crookedly.
'I've never seen eyes like yours, never.'

'And you've looked into a lot,' she said through her
teeth.

He kissed the corner of her mouth. 'Quite a few.
There's only been one who intrigued me as you do,
though. Her eyes were smoky blue and slanted, and she
looked at me through a thick curly tangle of lashes.'

Seared by jealousy of this unknown woman, she
snapped, 'Did you betray her, too?'

'No,' he said, and laughed, deep and soft in his throat.
'I helped her marry the man she loved.'

His scent drifted erotically into her nostrils, masculine, forbidden, tempting in so many ways; he was so
close that she could see the fine grain of his skin. In a

voice that was husky and slow she said, 'That doesn't sound like you.'

'Playing Cupid?' He laughed again and his mouth moved to her temple. 'No, I surprised myself with my altruism. But all it needed was a little jealousy.'

'Ah, that sounds more like it.' In spite of herself she was surrendering, her body curving towards him, lax, reacting to the warmth of his mouth, the soft blandishments of his kisses.

'Mmm. But even though I liked Oriel, she wasn't you. When I admired her long smoky eyes I looked for a blaze of tawny gold, and those exciting, mysterious stars. She was tall, not small and delicate, and she had black hair, not a wild coppery tangle that drifts like living silk across my skin.'

Sensual tension rippled between them, through them, in a rhythm she thought she had forgotten but knew now she had just repressed. Sighing, her mouth fuller and softer than it had been for years, she kissed his throat, the tip of her tongue resting for a trembling moment on the salty skin. His heartbeat raced, his arms about her tightened, and she was suddenly held prisoner in a cage formed of his strong thighs and iron arms, while his mouth plundered hers, revelling in the unbidden response he exacted from her.

He leaned back into the sofa, pulling her against his chest; she slid her hand through the front of his shirt and rested her head against his shoulder, using his strength as a lever, a refuge, a support, while their mouths mated in sweet fire and driving passion.

When he lifted his head he was smiling, his eyes hooded as they looked down into her slumbrous ones. 'You're magic,' he said, the words slurred. 'Rubies and fire and blood-red roses, rich crimson wine, all the dark bright hot things that smoulder behind the safe screens of convention.'

His hand shook slightly as it detailed the long curving line of her throat, hesitated for a moment, then followed that curve across the smooth material of her camisole top, cupping lightly, delicately, around her breast. She stiffened as fire streaked through her, pooling in the pit of her stomach, joining the conflagration at the fork of her body.

'Did you nurse Fleur, your little flower, at these breasts?' he asked, his thumb moving lightly, with refined torment, across the crowning peaks. 'I'd like to have seen that, Kate. Your child at your breast. When Brent was impregnating you did he make you shiver and sigh as I can? Was he as good a lover as I was? Did you sob out your hunger beneath him, writhing in an electric frenzy, and then arching tight as a drawn bow when the moment of ecstasy gripped you?'

She froze, and the bitterness of betrayal tasted like aloes in her mouth, in her heart. 'You'd think I'd learn,' she said, her voice infinitely weary as she straightened up, trying to pull away.

He held her there, his smile insolent on his handsome face. 'I've never forgotten,' he said softly. 'And it's still there, just as strong as it was that first time we saw each other. You know it. You feel it.'

'It's a snare and a delusion. Just like you.'

That brought the hateful mockery back. 'In what way, Kate?'

'Empty, hollow,' she said vehemently, wrestling to get free of him. He laughed, but let her go, and she got to her feet, running her trembling hands down her sides. 'I don't want this,' she said when she had recovered a little of her composure. She turned swiftly to where he sat, still leaning back, his head against the high back of the sofa, smiling, his eyes watching her from beneath his lowered lashes, his arrogant jaw lifted towards her.

'Possibly not.' He spoke slowly, the smile leaving his face. 'I don't particularly want it either. But it is there—

the fact that it's bloody inconvenient won't make it go away.'

'But we don't need to give in to it,' she pleaded distractedly.

'I think that's the problem.' He sat up and leaned his elbows on his knees, staring moodily into the fire. 'We've fought it all the way but that hasn't worked,' he said, looking up suddenly to catch her eyes pinned in helpless hunger on him. 'Perhaps we should try giving in to it.'

Sheer shock held her breathless for a long tense moment. She shook her head but before she could say anything he interrupted, speaking fast and persuasively. 'It's been eating at both of us all these years, the hunger, the need, the unbearable emptiness.'

'You want an affair.' Her voice was flat and heavy with pain.

He got up and strode across to where she stood immobile, his gait swift and tigerish. His hands caught her shoulders as he spoke fiercely, his eyes capturing hers. 'I want an end to looking for your eyes in another woman's face, to listening for your voice in every room I go into, to memories of a night that has haunted me ever since. You want it to be over, too, I can tell. The only reason we still want each other is because we only had that one night. Boredom, the eternal sameness of satiation, didn't have a chance to set in. I suggest we give boredom a chance. That way we might be free of each other at last.'

She shook her head. 'No. I'm not—I couldn't do that. I haven't got the strength—or the stamina.'

'You're afraid.'

'Yes,' she said simply, because it was the truth.

His hands fell away. 'I can accept that,' he said after a moment, his implacable face carved in stone, the only moving thing the leaping lights in his eyes and the barely moving lips saying incredible, humiliating words. 'But I'm not going to accept your refusal. I want you, and

I'm going to have you until I can look at you coolly, dispassionately, and assess you as just another woman I have slept with.'

She flinched, and he looked down at her as though seeing her for the first time. 'That's all I want,' he said beneath his breath. 'Then I can be whole again.'

She stepped away, sickened to her heart's core, and said stiffly, 'That's about the most bloody insulting thing you have ever said to me! I think it's time you went home.'

'Very well.' He went with her to the door, and said as she opened it. 'I'll ring you.'

'I don't want——'

He smiled and touched her cheek, in an oddly tender gesture. 'Kathy used to be a little more honest,' he said gently. 'She wanted, and wasn't ashamed of it. It was sheer hell not to respond to that innocent ardour.' His mouth twisted cynically. 'And just think, Kate, wouldn't you like to see me walk down the street and feel nothing, no fierce desire, no damned intolerable stirring in your loins, no hunger for a union that's a snare and a delusion?'

Rain slashed down as he disappeared out into the night. She watched the headlights of the Range Rover disappear down the drive and closed the door, shivering with more than cold. He would do it, she knew; he would hunt her down like tender prey, wear her out and sate himself in her, and when he was tired of all that she had to offer he would leave her and she would never see him again. And she would be left emotionally crippled.

Walking heavily, she went into the sitting-room and gathered up the cups, standing for a moment before the fire with his coffee-cup in her hand.

He had given her fair warning. He thought of her as a disease, something he had wrong with him, and he wanted to use her as a vaccination against herself. Perhaps he was right to think that only by sating their desire could they ever free themselves from the dark primeval spell, but that way lay pain unbearable for her.

Her lips stretched in a mirthless smile as she padded around tidying up, ridding her house, she realised, of any signs of his presence.

But he was right. Otherwise, why wasn't she married to any of the several men who had asked her in the last six years? Beginning with Brent. She sighed. He had sworn that he loved her enough for two, and she had been so exhausted, so shattered at the shambles she had made of her life, that she had almost given in. Only a bleak common sense had stopped her from making another ruinous mistake.

Eventually he had given up, and now he was living in Australia, happily married to a woman from Sydney, writing his fifth book. He had two children; they exchanged Christmas cards every year.

At last she had tidied everything up. The house was quiet around her, the small creaks and settlings blending with the rain on the roof and the hiss of the fire into a sound of domestic contentment. She looked around the warm cluttered room and felt an aching restlessness, a desire to run far and free with the wind in her face.

When she went in to check Fleur she found her cuddled under her blankets, her stuffed pony on the pillow. Bending, she gave the flushed cheek a soft kiss and left her, wondering how she was going to deal with the sudden avalanche fate had dumped on her. Nausea gripped her. Was it all going to start over again, the rollercoaster of emotions, the awful debilitating weakness that stopped her from salvaging any self-respect?

'No,' she said out loud as she went down the passage to her bedroom. 'No, and no and no, God help us both.'

Some days later she was forced to measure the sum of her newly aroused need by her anger when she realised that he wasn't going to contact her, that he had retained some small shred of sanity. With any luck he wasn't going to buy Kaurinui either.

But when she asked Mr Fairchild in the supermarket in Whitianga towards the end of the week, he looked a little surprised.

'Oh, yes, it's almost all through. André had to go back to town but his agent has been working with Mrs Cameron's lawyer, and I've had a couple of calls from André himself. Mentioned he knew you from some years back. Quite a man, isn't he?'

'Yes,' she said simply, embarrassed now.

'Well, you'll be able to renew his acquaintance. He's going to redo the homestead for us and build a massive new one on the bluff overlooking the creek.

Kate had been to the homestead several times, and had noted its age and state of genteel dilapidation. An old villa like her own, it clearly hadn't been touched for at least fifty years. The Camerons had not been good employers.

She said, 'Mrs Fairchild must be in seventh heaven.'

He grinned. 'Oh, yes, although she's not madly keen on living in it while it's being done. André suggested we move into a motel, but you have to live on a farm, it's not an eight-hour-day existence, so we'll stick it out. The architect will be in to see what she'd like done when everything's signed and sealed.

She hated herself for fishing, but she said casually, 'It sounds as though André's got great plans for the place.'

'No doubt about it. We're going bring in a lot of land that's been let go back, and refence the whole place, and he has plans for forestry and horticulture, as well as some tourism. I think he's thinking of doing something with the old mining trail that runs from behind your place to the kauri reserve back in the hills.'

'I thought that was dangerous.'

'Trail's OK,' he said cheerfully. 'Step off it in some parts and you might be in danger, but most trails here are like that. Those old gold-miners, they put shafts down all over the place.'

Kate had seen some of those shafts. Dark and ominous, they yawned beneath banks and through the bush and mountains over most of Coromandel, relics of the wild gold-mining days a century before. She said with a mental shudder, 'Well, I'd just as soon not have people tramping past my place. It might give Fleur ideas! She's already too interested for my peace of mind in that trail.'

The trail was recalled to her mind only too ominously several days later when Beth rang up and asked in a voice so elaborately casual that the strain rang through it, 'Have you seen Fergus and Sean?'

A cold worm of fear insinuated itself into Kate's consciousness. She looked out at the balmy weekend sunlight and said, 'No. No, I haven't. Why?'

CHAPTER EIGHT

'OH, THEY haven't been around for a couple of hours and Emma's just let slip that they've been planning an expedition all week.'

'Is that bad?'

'Yes.' Beth said grimly. 'It has to be to a place they know they're not allowed to go, otherwise why all the secrecy? They're not backward in coming forward when they need food for something like this! Emma said something about the gold-miners' trail at the back of your place.'

'Oh, lord.'

'Exactly. And Simon is not here, of course. Like all men he never is about when he's needed. He decided to take the day off to go fishing with a couple of mates.' But the lightly humorous note rang hollow.

'What can we do?'

'I'm going to ring the Fairchilds and see if they've seen sight or sign of them, and then I suppose I'll have to walk the trail. Can I leave Emma with you?'

'Yes, of course you can, but don't you think you should contact someone? The police?'

Beth said something that made Kate glad she was not one of the errant sons. 'Yes, I suppose I better had,' she added after a moment.

'And try not to worry too much,' Kate said grimly. 'In spite of everything, they're sensible kids.'

'I've been saying that for the last half-hour but it doesn't seem to help much.'

Kate put the receiver down and went to see if Fleur had heard anything about this 'expedition'. Defeated, she was on her way in again when the sound of the telephone set her running. It was Beth, and it was obvious that everything was all right.

'Mrs Fairchild had just seen them coming down the paddock,' she said. 'André is there so he's going to bring them back, and then I'm going to kill them.'

'Naturally. I'm so glad, Beth.'

'So am I. I wonder what on earth they—oh, I suppose they're growing up, but I wish they'd be a little more considerate of their mother while they're doing it. At this rate I'll be a little grey-haired lady before either of them has his first girlfriend!'

Kate's gurgle of laughter was echoed after a moment by Beth, who was ruefully aware that both boys already had girlfriends—or so their sister said. Hanging up the receiver, Kate thought that she was glad she was not the boys; Simon was inclined to be very strict with them, and they were likely to be severely punished. Still, they must have known this; no doubt weighed against the forbidden excitement of exploring the old trail punishment seemed a small price to pay.

And, aware that she was using the boys to keep her mind off the fact that André had returned, she went out into the humid warmth of the spring day and finished mowing the lawn. Then, hot and sticky, she and Fleur sat for a while listening to the birds call in the pear blossom, talking with the idle inconsequence of old friends.

Unconsciously of course she was listening for the sound of the Range Rover; as the warm afternoon slid smoothly towards the evening she realised with what she convinced herself was satisfaction that he must have taken the boys down and gone straight back to Kaurinui.

She was pulling weeds from beneath the azaleas when the distinctive note of an engine made her realise how wrong she had been. As it progressed briskly up the steep pitch of the drive Fleur came running out of the house, her face alive with pleasure.

'Mr Hunter!' she shouted, and to Kate's astonishment flung herself into his arms. To her even greater astonishment he lifted the child up and gave her eager face a warm kiss.

'Mummy said you prob'ly weren't coming back,' she said, slanting her mother a look that combined glee and reproach.

He set her down carefully and said with sardonic amusement, 'Oh, Mummy knows better than that.'

'How long are you going to stay this time?'

'For a while.'

Kate decided that it was time to put a stop to this touching scene. He might enjoy enslaving her daughter on a whim but he should realise that she would be shattered if he treated her as a toy. Fleur loved deeply when she loved.

Scrambling to her feet, she said crisply, 'But you're going to be very busy, aren't you, Mr Hunter?'

'Not too busy to visit you,' he said promptly, his eyes gleaming with sly amusement as they took in her irritation.

'Can you come and have tea with us?' Fleur demanded.

'Not tonight, sweetheart, I'm going out.' André smiled into the little girl's earnest face. 'Perhaps Mummy can bring you up some time to see some little kunekune pigs Mr Fairchild's got,' he said casually.

So angry that she could barely speak, Kate intervened. 'Some day, perhaps,' she said smoothly, her eyes narrowing as she dared him to pursue the matter further.

'What's kune-thingy pigs?' Fleur looked interested.

Ignoring Kate's anger and contempt, André squatted down beside the little girl. 'Cute little fat black piglets, with furry bodies. Nobody knows quite where they came from; some people say they came all the way from

Malaysia, but they've been in New Zealand for a long time, from the very earliest days. There aren't many around now, but Mr Fairchild got two off a man who has a small herd. You'd like them. They eat carrots from your hands.'

Fleur's face lit up. 'Really truly?'

'Really truly,' he assured her gravely.

'Mummy, can we go up today to see them?'

Kate cast a cool, glittering glance at the man who had no hesitation in using a small girl to further his own ends, and said serenely, 'Not today, Fleur. Perhaps another day. Say goodbye to Mr Hunter, he's going now.'

At this summary dismissal he tossed her a smile that promised retribution, but made no audible protest. Preoccupied with thoughts of the pigs, Fleur gave him a charming absent smile and waved him off, leaving Kate to watch him go with a bewildering mixture of anger at his unashamed manipulation of her daughter and a treacherous delight to which she refused to admit.

Unfortunately Fleur's desire to see the pigs didn't dissipate during the next week. She never failed to mention them after school, and Kate, who had been out to dinner twice and found herself sitting by André both times, was angry and disappointed by his exploitation of the child's affection for him.

Every bit as irritating was his obvious social success. Of course any hostess would be thrilled by an unattached male of his manifold attractions, but it was humiliating to have to watch the efforts, subtle and obvious, of an assortment of women to attach him. And André was his normal enigmatic self, bland, charming, ironic, the essential male danger of the man almost hidden by the social façade.

It was infuriating. But worse than that was the effect his presence in the district had on Kate. Oh, she managed to control her wayward emotions during the day although her appetite became erratic, but at night she slept poorly and twice she woke from dreams where sensuality and fear were joined in a disturbing blend.

Her mood was not helped when after a particularly depressing day spent fitting one of her least liked clients while being forced to endure a long spiel on his eminently desirable characteristics, interspersed with not very subtle questions on where she had met him before, she was faced with a daughter who bounded in after school to tell her that one of her small friends had visited the piglets and declared they were 'choice', higher praise than which there was none.

'Can we go up tonight, Mummy?' she pleaded, throwing her schoolbag on to the chair and grabbing an apple from the bowl. 'You promised we could, you know you did.'

Mentally consigning André to the lowest portion of hell, Kate said cheerfully, 'No, not tonight, darling.'

But, normally the most reasonable of children, Fleur chose this occasion to dig her heels in. 'But, Mummy, I want to go, and you said we could. You *promised*, Mummy, you know you did.'

'And we will go, when it's a suitable time,' Kate said imperturbably as she sliced potatoes for a hot-pot.

A suitable time was when André was back in Auckland.

'Why not tonight?' Fleur whined, kicking her heels on the chair.

'Because it's going to rain again. Look out the window, it's been raining all day and the clouds are still hanging heavy on the hills. The weather report is for showers, some heavy, and thunder, at least until tomorrow. So it will be silly to go up the valley tonight and get wet, won't it?'

But Fleur was not to be appeased. 'I want to go now,' she said, something in her voice reminding Kate of André at his most autocratic. Then she changed tactics, smiling winningly. 'Mummy, you don't have to come. I can go by myself. I can walk over the hill on the mine trail, just like Fergus and Sean did. I'll be under the trees so it won't matter if it rains.'

'Darling, don't be silly. That mine trail is dangerous. There are mine shafts everywhere——'

'But Sean said it's quite safe——'

'No,' Kate said sharply. 'If I ever find you've been on that trail I'll be extremely angry, Fleur. It is truly dangerous, darling, you know that. Fergus and Sean got into severe trouble when they walked over it.'

Fleur flung her apple on to the floor and flounced off the chair. They had a sharp tussle of wills which ended in Fleur picking up the apple, but she refused to be reasoned or coaxed into a better humour and eventually took herself off with an audible sniff that hinted of tears to be shed in the privacy of her room.

Kate spent a vindictive five minutes or so dreaming up punishments for men who involved small girls in their private battles. When the hot-pot was safely cooking she eyed the doorway to the bedroom wing, but forced herself to stay away. Eventually Fleur would get over her tantrum and emerge; experience had proved that, until then, she was best left to herself.

Morosely, Kate went back into the kitchen and prepared her daughter's favourite pudding, a jelly whipped with cream and egg whites.

Then she went into the office and glowered at the dress she was making. Her client wanted several alterations which would ruin the line. Finally, she said aloud, 'Oh, what the hell? She has to wear it,' and set to work on them.

When, some time later, she arrived back in the sitting-room, she stopped in surprise. The door to the bedroom wing was still firmly closed. Retiring to lick your wounds was one thing, she decided, glancing at her watch, but sulking was another thing entirely.

She opened the door and called, 'Fleur.'

No answer. She tried again, and when there was still no answer went along to her daughter's bedroom and knocked on the door. Silence. Her heart gave a funny jump; she turned the handle and looked inside.

Fleur was not there.

A cold sensation squeezed her heart. 'Fleur, don't be silly. Come on out now.'

Although she knew Fleur was not in the room she went through it swiftly, and then the rest of the house. Still no Fleur. She stood in the doorway and called, and then recalled her daughter's threat to walk over the mine trail.

Kate stared across the short grass to the boundary, hoping against hope that she would see a small figure in a yellow rainslicker. But the hillside was ominously bare, and beyond the grass the bush frowned down, the branches dripping and dense. Stupidly she ran again into Fleur's bedroom, but its emptiness frightened her. Don't panic, she adjured herself fiercely. She went out and searched across the lawn. Sure enough, by the fence was a footprint in the mud. The chill around her heart intensified.

'Well, it looks as though the little monkey set off on her own to see the kunekune,' she said in a tight, uneven voice as she ran back inside. With trembling fingers she dialled the number of the Kaurinui homestead.

It was André who answered. Stammering slightly, she asked if he had seen any sign of Fleur.

'No.' His voice was sharp and cool. 'Why?'

'I—she wanted to see the kunekune piglets. We had a bit of a battle about it.'

There was a tense silence and then his voice bit out an expletive. 'I'm sorry,' he said heavily. 'It never occurred to me—God, Kate, I'm sorry! But what makes you think she might have set out to walk all this way?'

She said in a half-sob, 'When I wouldn't bring her to see the piglets she said she'd walk over the old mine trail like the Beatson brothers. Naturally I f-forbade her to even think of it! Usually after a difference of opinion she goes to her room to read herself out of her temper. When she didn't come out I searched through the house and around the yard. There's a print of her gumboot in the mud by the fence.'

His voice altered, became incisive and calm. 'All right. Jim's not here, he's been off at a sale all day. I'll start out from this end and see if I can see her. She won't get lost if she sticks to the trail.'

'I'll set off from this end.'

'Be careful,' he said automatically.

'Yes.' She forced back tears. 'You too. The hillside is littered with mine shafts.'

His voice was wonderfully reassuring. 'Kate, can you imagine Fleur going into a dark hole anywhere?'

She managed a shaky laugh. 'No, I suppose not.'

'That's my sensible Kate. Make sure you're wrapped up warmly,' he commanded. 'You'd better bring some extra clothes for her, too. It's raining on the tops here.'

Stuffing a thermos of hot soup into her backpack, Kate's fingers fumbled, her face bleak as she thought of those hills, honeycombed with shafts. But André was right; adventurous as Fleur was, she wouldn't dream of going anywhere near a dank hole in a bank. Clinging to that thought, she hauled on warm clothes.

Once clad in thick corduroy trousers, a woollen shirt, and a Swanndri jacket, she pulled on her boots and raincoat. As she started up the hill, torch clutched in her hand, a coil of thin strong cord wound around her waist, she thought grimly of the scolding she was going to give her daughter when she found her.

The cloud had settled further down on to the hills like a smothering blanket. It was still dry on the lower slopes but it wouldn't be long before the rain reached them. Half an hour, she thought, trying to take her mind off a mental picture of her daughter lost and terrified. How far could she go in half an hour? A kilometre? Possibly even more. Fleur could run like a goat when she wanted to. Still, for the first kilometre or so the track was steep and muddy so she couldn't have got too far ahead.

With a set face she climbed the fence and plunged into the great silence of the bush. It was very still, the tall trees looming through a light mist, while down on the floor the treeferns and thick tangled undergrowth cut out most of the light. As she strode up the rutted, muddy trail Kate looked from side to side, calling steadily. The growth was so dense that a small girl need only be twenty feet away to be completely invisible. Twice she found small footprints in the mud, but as she got further into the bush the trail became matted with dead and decaying leaves, the fibrous matter making it difficult to see if anyone had passed over it.

Her voice robbed of resonance by the all-pervading dampness, she continued to shout Fleur's name, managing to keep the note of desperation under strict control. She heard the rain before it actually arrived, realising with a sinking heart that it was one of the increasingly heavy showers that had plagued them for the last ten days. All too soon she was walking through drips as big as bullets, exploding into cacophony as they hit her raincoat and face, the noise drowning out any other sounds. Slowing, she pushed the hood of her jacket back from her head, straining her ears in case she missed an answering call. In spite of the dense canopy far above the rain stung the tender skin of her face.

It was so dark she considered switching on the torch, but the prospect of using up the batteries kept it unlit. Not even to herself would she admit that the light might yet prove to be vital. Occasionally she passed a bank where the dark hole of a mine shaft crouched, its very menace easing her fears a little. There was no way she could imagine Fleur entering one of those, not for any reason.

She was making her way towards a grove of kauri trees, their huge straight trunks stretching up into the mist like dinosaurs' legs, when she heard an echo. Panting, her heart rocketing in her chest, she stopped. Could it be André?

No, she thought, a sudden surge of hope lighting her eyes, he wouldn't have had time to reach this far. She had been walking for twenty minutes, and still hadn't got over the top of the ridge.

But it was him; he loomed out of the rain looking totally at home in the primeval landscape, his face etched into lines as grim as hers above dark workmanlike oilskins. Like her, he had pushed the hood back the better to hear and his wet hair was sleek and black against the finely shaped head.

'No sign?'

Disappointment and a fear more intense than anything she had ever experienced clogged her throat. Until that moment she hadn't realised how convinced she had been that he would find their daughter.

'How—how did you get here so quickly?' she croaked.

'I couldn't see her walking more than a couple of kilometres in the time available, so I brought the Range Rover to the end of the side trail at the top of the hill and walked in from there,' he explained.

She nodded, swallowing because her throat was aching with terror. 'What do we do now?'

'I suggest we go back to the side trail and start again. There is no way she could have got beyond the junction. And this time, you call. She may not have recognised my voice, or, if she did, wanted to answer me.'

'She likes you.' The words were blurted out. 'It's me she probably won't answer. I wouldn't take her to see your piglets—that's why she set off.'

'If anyone's to blame it's me,' he said, self-contempt sharpening the words. 'I set you up, deliberately and without a thought—I should bloody well be shot!'

She bit her lip, impelled by an odd need to comfort him. However, he turned around, once more in control. 'Well, recriminations can come later, when we've found her; at the moment it's sheer self-indulgence to wallow in them. Comfort yourself with the thought of the scolding you're going to give her when we find her.'

Numbly she nodded again. 'Yes, only I'm afraid I'll be too relieved to be cross.'

'I have it on the best of authority—my stepmother's—that the greater the fear, the greater the anger. Have you let anyone else know?'

'Yes. I rang Beth, and she's going to call the police and go up to the house in case Fleur c-comes back by herself.'

So dark as to be almost black, his eyes searched her face, probing beneath the fragile composure. 'Good. Don't look so tragic, Kate. If she's up here we'll find her.'

Insensibly comforted, she essayed a smile. It didn't quite come off but his green gaze softened. 'That's better,' he said half beneath his breath. 'Let's get going.'

Before it gets dark, her mind supplied.

Wearily she trudged beside him up through the mud and the rain and the brooding impersonal beauty of the bush. They shouted Fleur's name, taking it in turns, and calling especially loudly down the entrance to each mine shaft they came across.

If André noticed that she winced every time they did this he made no comment. At least, she thought once, the track was easy to follow. There was no temptation to wander off it. It was a double-edged consolation. She didn't know which was worse: the thought of her daughter, so quick and bright and eager, crouching terrified in one of the dark holes crying for her mother, or of her being lost in the huge expanse of the ranges, wandering hopelessly until her strength—and possibly her life—gave out.

Exposure had always been a distinct possibility; if she wasn't found soon it would become inevitable.

Kate's voice rasped and broke. Drawing a ragged breath, she controlled it as she called again. But her thoughts, chasing themselves feverishly about her brain, were not so easily controlled. Morbidly, she found herself thinking that this was her punishment for not telling André that Fleur was his daughter. She had been selfish and frightened, and she was being punished for it.

Even as the last remnants of logic in her brain told her she was being hysterical she heard to her horror a child's wail echoing up from the bowels of the earth.

'Mummy...Mummy...'

Kate sagged, saved from falling by André's strong arm whipping around her shoulders. 'Answer her,' he ordered roughly.

The entrance to the mine shaft was small, under an overhang of rock, but it was clear that the constant rain of this wettest of winters had undermined the ground, which was soft and boggy, with signs of a recent cave-in. Kate thrust her head into its dank depths. Her voice sounded strange, thick and muffled and echoing. 'Fleur, darling, are you all right?'

'Mummy!' She began to cry, hopeless choking sobs, and Kate reacted entirely on instinct, tearing at the mouth of the hole, desperate to reach and comfort her daughter.

'No!' André's hard, hurtful hands yanked her back. 'You're not going down there, it's too dangerous.'

'Oh, God,' she whispered, struggling. 'I have to go, damn you! She's frightened—can't you hear she's petrified down there in the dark——?'

He shook her into silence, his dark face intimidating. 'You won't help her by losing control,' he bit out. 'Call to her, tell her I'm here and I'll be coming down to find her.' He finished with another shake, watching as the rough treatment cleared away the panic in her wan face.

She caught her breath in a sob. 'Yes, I'm sorry. Of course.' Turning back to the obscene hole, she called out in a voice that barely deviated from evenness, 'Fleur, it's Mummy. Stop crying, sweetheart. I can't hear what you're saying. Have you hurt yourself?'

'My leg's sore. Mummy, I don't like the dark, I want to go home...' Her voice eddied and echoed, the black walls of the earth robbing it of humanity, making it difficult to understand. Kate had to listen intently to make sense of the words.

'I know, sweetheart.' Whitefaced, she leaned further in, hating the stifling darkness, striving to push it away for her daughter with her words. 'Fleur, listen, darling. Mr Hunter is coming down to get you. OK?'

Fleur's sobs redoubled, combining with the echoes to produce a shattering turbulence in which nothing could be heard.

'Stop that!' Kate ordered, making her voice stern.

Slowly the sobbing quietened.

'Mr Hunter is coming down,' Kate said slowly, trying to pitch her voice for absolute clarity. 'OK?'

'Yes I'm cold, Mummy, and my leg hurts.'

'Ask her if she can see you, or the light.'

Fleur's voice was a little less anguished as she answered. 'I can see a light but it's a long way away.'

'All right, don't worry, we'll have you out in a very short time.' In a voice devoid of expression she relayed this to a grim-faced André as he freed himself of his oilskins and jersey, dragging a coil of rope from his pack. Quickly, efficiently, he tied one end of the rope to a sturdy tree, then belayed the other end around his waist. 'Tell her I'm coming now,' he said.

Kate complied. Fleur said tearfully, 'OK.'

As he crouched in the mouth of the shaft, his eyes were a pure blazing green. He looked at Kate's white agonised face. 'I'll get her out,' he promised.

She swallowed, and nodded. If it was humanly possible he would. Before the tension in her expression had a chance to ease he went on quickly and clearly, 'If you don't hear anything from me in fifteen minutes, mark the shaft with my coat and get the hell off down the hill to raise the alarm. Search and Rescue and the police will know what to do.'

Her whole face expressed her revulsion, but she nodded again, then, impelled by some strange need, reached out a hand and touched his face. 'Take care, André.' It was all she could bring herself to say, but for a moment he smiled, that reckless, slashing grin she had known of old, and his mouth clung for a second to her cold fingers.

'See you, darling,' he said, and eased himself into the hole.

She had never known how difficult it was to wait. Occasionally she heard him call a comment, whether down to Fleur or up to her she didn't know; for some reason, now that he was in the shaft, she could no longer hear the actual words he said, or Fleur's answer, while the acoustics made it impossible to tell the tone of their voices.

All she could do was look at the rope, her heart leaping with terror every time there was a tug or a pull, impelling her to her feet to make sure his very professional-looking knots were holding.

As of course they were.

The rain eased, the huge drops coming further apart and then slackening almost entirely, but the dusk crept slowly, inexorably down through the trees. High above her a tui sang, and then another bird, its soft warblings obscurely comforting. Kate looked at her watch for the fiftieth time, and killed an impulse to scream down the dank black shaft.

Some time during that endless period of waiting she realised she would have to tell André that Fleur was his daughter. She didn't need to think the decision through; it was just necessary, something she had to do.

And then, when her strained nerves were at snapping point, she heard their voices, still muffled, but much closer, and knew that they were on their way out. First Fleur, her little face bruised and streaked with blood from grazes, closely followed by a filthy André, but, mercifully, through all the mud flashed two identical grins, gay and insouciant, that spark of recklessness only just under control.

Kate drew a deep breath, then a smile of radiant joy trembled across her face and she dropped to her knees, hugging her daughter to her with arms that hurt. Fleur burst into tears. 'I won't be naughty again,' she wept, pressing her face into her mother's breast. 'I promise I won't. I didn't want to make you cry, Mummy.'

Unaware that the tears were streaking her face, Kate murmured, 'All right, sweetheart, it's all right.' With the child in her arms she stood up and turned to André, her eyes luminous and transparent. 'Thank you,' she whispered, extending the magic circle of her embrace to take him in.

His arm came about her shoulders; Fleur looped hers about his neck and pulled his head close to theirs, so that she could kiss them both.

Inevitably, André's head turned; he kissed Kate, and for a moment the incandescent joy of reunion was transmuted into the flare of passion she had so hated.

'Gratitude?' he asked harshly as he pulled himself away.

Some of the radiance dimmed in her expression but she met his savage glance with steady composure. 'Would you like me to be ungrateful?'

His mouth kicked up at once corner. 'No, of course not. However, now that the initial transports of joy are over, I suggest we get back to the house where we can get this filthy scrap into a bath. The quickest way to go will be down to the Range Rover; I'll ring the house from there and let them know we've found them.'

'You have a telephone in your Range Rover?' she asked incredulously.

'A friend's idea of a joke,' he returned smoothly, slinging his oilskin over his shoulders and extending a hand to Fleur. 'Come on, angel, let's get you home and dry.'

'I'll carry her.' Kate felt she would never be able to bear to put her down again.

'She's too heavy. Besides, you can walk, can't you, Fleur? There's nothing wrong with her beyond a few bruises and grazes.'

'And shock!'

His eyes gleamed mockingly. 'I'd say that you are the one who's closest to shock. Fleur knew we'd find her, didn't you, sweetheart?'

Fleur looked from her mother to her father, and nodded. 'Yes,' she said with all the simple trust of a happy child. 'I knew you would.'

'So, let's get going.'

He was right. Fleur walked, her small paw clutched in Kate's, her spirits rapidly recovering to their normal high level. She told them how she had stepped under the bank to get out of the rain and how the weakened ground had collapsed beneath her feet, precipitating her down a steep slope in the darkness of the shaft. From the bottom she could not see how to get back to the dim light she could discern in the distance above her, so after a fruitless search for a dry patch of ground she had huddled where she could see the light.

It had seemed like forever, but she knew they would come, she told them artlessly, and then she heard them calling. That had been the best part, unless it was when she heard André make his way down the slope, saw his torch bobbing, and felt his arms about her at last.

The two adults exchanged looks above her head. Clearly she hadn't heard André's first call. Kate passed a hand over the rough wet head, and found a slight bump above one ear. It shouldn't have been a hard enough blow to render her unconscious, but she would have to be checked by a doctor. And, just in case, it might be a good idea not to give her anything to eat or drink.

She certainly didn't seem concussed, however. In fact, with childhood's buoyant optimism, she seemed disposed to treat the whole incident as an enormous adventure. Kate grimaced wryly, but encouraged this outlook, forbearing to scold or censure just yet.

Once in the Range Rover André used the telephone to call the house and tell Beth that they had found her, and that they were going to take her in to the doctor immediately.

'Thank God,' Beth said fervently. 'I'll head off home then, where I'll kill Fergus and Sean all over again for putting the idea into her head, bless her.'

Choking back a tearful chuckle, Kate said, 'No, don't—they weren't to know. Thanks, Beth.'

André put the vehicle into gear and set off along the narrow winding road, driving fast but skilfully. Within a short time they were at the doctor's surgery, and in an even shorter time Fleur had been X-rayed and pronounced fit and well, her grazes disinfected and cleaned, her face cleared of its layer of mud and tears and blood.

'Don't,' the doctor, father of three, said sternly, 'ever do such a thing again, will you?'

Her eyes enormous, she shook her head and clutched André's hand. The doctor looked from one to the other, and Kate's heart beat a rapid tattoo. However, he said nothing, merely adding in a milder voice, 'Keep an eye on her, and if you see anything you don't like the look of, don't hesitate to ring me.'

At home, by then a little cocksure, Fleur announced that she wanted to watch television. 'No,' Kate said mildly. 'You're having a bath and then a small snack, and then, sweetheart, you're going to bed.'

She protested, but when it was interrupted by a yawn she changed it to a demand that André come to see her in her bath. He grinned and agreed, and she went off happily, all horrors safely in the past. As she supervised her bath and washed the thick muddy locks Kate found herself wishing that her own fears were as easy to forget.

When André arrived they played a hectic game of submarines, then he wiped the bathroom down while Kate dried the small pink body and thrust her into her favourite green and gold pyjamas. 'All right?' she asked, kissing her nose.

Fleur gave the heart-wrenching grin so like her father's. 'Yes, only I'm awfully tired, Mummy. Can I have some soup? And then you can read a story to me and then I'll go to bed.'

While she was waiting Beth had made some fluffy scones to go with the hot-pot simmering on the back of the stove, so they all ate, and when Fleur's eyelids drooped over her eyes Kate took her off to bed. The story was short, and by the time it was finished the child was asleep, her face as innocent and smooth as though she had spent an ordinary day.

Kate's eyes were suspiciously moist as she pulled the blanket over the small form; she stood for a long moment looking down at her. So small, so valiant, so dearly loved...

But she couldn't put off the moment when she had to confront André alone once more. He had showered and changed his clothes for some he had stowed in the back of the Range Rover, and was standing in front of the fire when she went into the room, his arm along the mantel, looking down into the flames. His profile was severe, all straight lines and aristocratic angles, with only the curves of his mouth to soften the forbidding strength. He didn't seem to hear her arrival, for he stood motionless, the fluid power of his body held in stasis. Beneath the olive-green shirt she could see the muscles of his shoulders and arms, the smooth bulges and contours in a singing symmetry of strength and power. For all his leanness, André was incredibly strong.

Before she had time to change her mind, she said starkly, 'Fleur is your daughter.'

He didn't move. Not a muscle quivered in his face. Then he straightened, and his lashes drooped, hiding his thoughts as effectively as shutters over a window.

'Really?' His voice was blank, smooth as cream.

Whatever she had expected it wasn't this. She said thinly, 'Yes.'

'Born, I presume, of the one night of love we shared, before you ran away and jumped into Sheridan's bed.' His tone invested the words with a mockery that didn't hide the cold distaste beneath it.

'I didn't,' she said through her teeth, 'jump into his bed. That's how I know that Fleur is your daughter, not his.'

'I see.' He lifted his lashes and looked directly at her, his eyes as hard and sharp as quartz splinters. 'What made you decide to tell me this now, Kate?'

'What happened this afternoon.' She struggled for composure but managed only to produce a kind of flat, take-it-or-leave-it tone that even to her didn't sound truthful. 'It suddenly didn't seem fair that she doesn't know her own father, and you didn't realise that you had a daughter. And—I know this is completely irrational, but I thought I was being punished for being a coward and not telling you.'

Silence. The firelight flickered ominously on the chiselled features of the man who watched her patiently, like a great predator, lean and tense with the desire to kill. At last he said calmly, 'Or perhaps it was when you realised that instead of being merely well-off I am now *excessively* rich?'

Colour fled from her skin at the sound of her own derisive words, spoken to Beth on the night of the barbecue, flung back at her. She began to see the way his mind was working. 'No,' she said haughtily. 'I don't need your money, thank you. I can keep us.'

'But a little extra would be welcome, I imagine.'

She scanned the classic lines of his face, her eyes sparkling with rage yet cold, very cold. 'No,' she said curtly. 'You imagine wrong.'

His mouth tightened. 'So you thought you'd do something for your daughter, provide her——'

'No!' She took a furious step towards him, her expression convulsed with rage, but his ferocious restraint, his self-control, stopped her.

'I've always felt that I could never hit a woman,' he remarked almost conversationally, 'but if you hit me I might feel constrained to hit back. So, what do you want me to do about Fleur?'

'Nothing,' she said shortly, angry because somewhere deep inside she was fighting a crippling sense of disappointment. 'I just thought you should know.'

He swung away from the mantel and came towards her, a darkly lethal threat, and smiled when she took an involuntary step backwards. 'Yes, you might well feel a little alarmed,' he said in the soft voice of ultimate rage. 'However, I wouldn't soil my fingers with you.'

Stunned, she saw him veer towards the door and disappear through it; as the rain came pouring suddenly down again the outer door of the house crashed to. A moment later she saw the lights of the Range Rover hurtle down the drive and turn at the base of the hill up to Kaurinui.

She went out and locked the door, then came back and sat down by the fire, her face bleak and drawn as she realised what she had just done.

CHAPTER NINE

DAWN found Kate sitting in front of a dead fire, her hand cupping the side of her face as she stared into the grey embers with desolate eyes. She listened to the sounds of the birds outside and wondered whether there was anyone else in the world who had managed to make such a mess of her life.

And not just once. Once could be excused. As Fiona had said all those years ago, 'Every woman needs a tragic love-affair in her past.'

When Kate first met André she had been so innocent it made her heart ache to think of that younger self. She hadn't had a prayer when he turned the full force of his masculine sensuality on to her.

His subsequent betrayal had forced her to choose: either to hide, or to surrender. She had chosen to hide, instinctively knowing that she would lose something vital in herself if she yielded to the pain.

Looking back, she realised now that she had opted for safety. The anguish she had suffered had frozen her emotions; subconsciously she had made the decision never to allow herself to feel so deeply again. And, except for her love for Fleur, she had kept that bargain with herself. She had used her work and her child and the day-to-day struggles to survive as a buffer against feeling too much, against life itself.

It had been self-serving and petty. As was refusing to tell André that she had borne his daughter. Wounded and resentful, she had punished him in the only way she could, but there had been too much unfinished business between her and André for her tactics to work; her flight left too much unsaid.

In the dark bitter reaches of the night she had faced unpalatable facts; it was time, she thought wearily, to face another, the bitterest, most agonising of all.

She still loved André Hunter. All those years ago she had fallen so deeply in love with him that somehow it had been chiselled into her soul. Other adolescents got over their crushes. Trust me, she thought ironically, to become fixated on a man who first betrayed me and now has every reason to despise me.

So much for her assumption that it was just sex. Just! She got to her feet, walking mechanically with none of her usual grace. Sunlight was streaming into the kitchen; she filled the kettle and stood watching a fantail catch breakfast in the tea-tree bush outside the window, its triangular tail moving with sharp little jerks as it slew untold invisible insects among the rosy crinkled flowers.

Perhaps André had been right when he said they should sate themselves in the overwhelming passion that marked their relationship.

But even as she accepted the cynical thought she knew that such a relationship would kill an essential part of her. In fact, that was why her sense of self-preservation had urged her to flee after the night Fleur was conceived. Over the intervening years she had thought she had grown up, put the tempestuous, passionate aberration that was her love behind her where it belonged, in her adolescent years.

Well, it had come back, she thought grimly, and because of its long repression it was stronger than ever. She had only to look at him to want him, only hear his voice to feel her skin pull tightly over a body that ached with hungers she dared not yield to. Devil that he was, rash and unscrupulous, wicked, taunting devil, she loved him. It was as easy and as hard as that.

But what was she going to do about it?

She was sipping coffee in the breakfast alcove when Fleur appeared, slightly shamefaced, shooting wary glances from beneath her thick straight lashes.

'Right, let's get ready for the day,' Kate said briskly.

'Am I going to school?'

She eyed her daughter sternly. 'Why not?'

Fleur opened her mouth, then closed it. Yes, she was André's daughter, but she knew when not to push her luck any further.

The week that followed was calm, almost placid. Kate discovered at the store, that central clearing-house for village information, that André had left the night of Fleur's escapade and no one knew when he was expected back. Running, she thought with a certain grim satisfaction, knowing that he would return when he had made up his mind what to do.

Fleur recovered from her fright, accepted her punishment with the good grace of one who knew it had been deserved, and asked constantly after André.

On Friday evening they went into town to buy a pair of shoes for Fleur, and came across Jim Fairchild. Fleur danced up to him and asked, 'Are the kunekune pigs still at your place, Mr Fairchild?'

He looked enquiringly at Kate, relaxing at her tiny nod. 'Yes,' he said, looking down at the child's vivid face. 'But don't you set out to see them again, will you?'

Fleur pulled a face. 'No,' she said with such earnestness that both adults had to hide a smile. 'Is Mr Hunter with you?'

Jim shook his head. 'No, he's a busy man, he has to work in Auckland.'

Fleur's face fell. 'When's he coming back?'

He hesitated for a moment, his mild gaze sliding sideways. 'Not for a couple of weeks or so.'

'Oh.' She made a quick recovery. 'Mummy, can we go tomorrow if it's fine and see the pigs?'

Kate smiled. 'I don't see why not.' She looked across at Jim, surprising an expression of something like guilt on his face. 'What time would be most suitable for you?'

'Oh, any time,' he said a little awkwardly. 'How about lunchtime? Mary said I was to make sure you came for a meal when you came.'

'Lovely. I'll ring tonight, shall I, to check that it's all right with her?' She flashed him a sweet, rather mischievous smile, the elusive dimple much in evidence.

'Oh, well, yes, I suppose you'd better clear it with the boss,' he returned, grinning.

Saturday was fine and clear, not polished with the cold clarity of winter but humming with a warm expectancy that reminded her that spring was there and summer just around the corner. Not that spring was a fixed season in this corner of New Zealand, when jonquils bloomed in July, and September, the official opening month of the season, was often the coldest and wettest of the year. But as Kate looked at the tui singing in the white blossoms of the pear tree in the back yard, she felt a refreshment of her spirits, an upwelling of joy and delight from some deep unfound place inside her.

She was singing as she swung the car into the gate at Kaurinui, Fleur's voice lifted high in concert with hers. But her voice broke off in mid-note, for beside the big farm tractor was André's Range Rover. And there, coming through the gate from the house, was the man himself, tall and lean, clad in jungle-green safari trousers with a striped drill shirt beneath a cotton sweatshirt, the fickle sun coaxing red highlights from the dark hair. He should have looked out of place, citified, in his well-cut casual clothes, but with his facility for dominating any situation he was perfectly at home in the wild landscape.

Kate watched him narrowly, rather shocked at her wry resignation.

'Mr Hunter!' Fleur waved madly.

He grinned, and came towards them, his mocking glance directing a challenge at Kate. Instantly her energies surged into life; as with no one else, she felt vividly, vitally alive.

'I thought you were in Auckland,' she observed crisply as he opened her door.

'I came back.'

He helped her out, his fingers on her arm with an almost insulting possessiveness, and smiled down into her tense face. His eyes were amused but there was no softness there. Well, she asked herself as he turned away to greet Fleur, what did you expect? Gentleness? He is not a gentle man.

Fleur kissed him fervently, clambering about him like a young puppy; as Kate watched them together she thought that he was good with young ones, casual yet not bored, affectionate and firm at the same time. No wonder Fleur adored him. She watched them closely, looking for a change in his attitude towards the child, now that he had been told she was his daughter.

But whatever his emotions he was giving nothing away, and the narrow smile he directed at her when he looked up and caught her watching was mirthless and edged with mockery.

Don't go spinning dreams, she adjured herself sharply, turning away.

'I'm afraid Mummy and I have to go out,' he remarked as he ushered them up to the house. Ignoring Kate's stunned, wary glance he went on blandly, 'But Mrs Fairchild would like you to stay here.'

Fleur viewed them suspiciously. 'Why can't I come with you?'

'I thought you wanted to see the piglets? You might like to go for a ride on the pony, too. And there are lambs and calves, and even a few chicks, I believe.'

Perhaps it was the chicks that turned the scales, but Fleur forgot all about going with them in a babble of excited anticipation.

His fingers on Kate's arm were inexorable. She listened to Fleur with a kind of inevitability, accepting that she owed him this.

Mrs Fairchild met them at the door, her curiosity well hidden; it was clear that like everyone else in the Coromandel she was prepared to idolise her employer. Kate ordered herself not to be waspish and tried to behave normally.

Five minutes later they were in the Range Rover, waving goodbye to an excited small girl who didn't even wait for them to disappear before pulling Mrs Fairchild towards the orchard where the piglets lived with their mother. Stifling an odd regretful sigh, and firmly quelling the flock of butterflies in her stomach, Kate turned her eyes back to the view through the windscreen.

He took her up a farm track to a small plateau on the side of one of Coromandel's high hills; at some stage it had been cleared and grassed, and now formed a paddock surrounded by bush. In the front it dropped away a little so that above the trees one could see across the fertile green coastal plain to the sea, and the Mercury islands offshore, glowing in the spring sunlight like jewels through thin gauze.

She said quietly, 'It reminds me of your bach at Whangaroa.'

'Yes,' he admitted. 'I seem to have a need for high places. I may build another eyrie here.'

'Do you no longer have the one up north?'

His mouth twisted, whether in pain or irony it was hard to tell. 'No, I sold it after I took you there.'

She shot him a quick glance, but his profile was unrevealing and her eyes moved back to the view. Stress pulled her nerves awry. She tried to relax, to calm her feverish pulse by deep breathing, but she was too strung up to pay any attention to the view. It was with relief that she realised that for once he seemed prepared to put off confrontation.

'I don't know whether it's dry enough to put a rug on the grass,' he said, 'but if we spread out the food on the tray of the 'Rover I've got shooting sticks we can use to sit on.'

So they did that. She too was prepared to wait, to fortify herself before she spoke of the years they had spent apart.

Mrs Fairchild had surpassed herself; there were pâté and crusty farmhouse bread, cheeses and avocado and small sweet tomatoes, and a selection of salads as well as cold sliced meat. To follow she had packed fruit, bananas, and mandarins from Tauranga, and, to Kate's amusement, a ripe pineapple.

All in all, a feast. If she hadn't been so unsettled Kate would have enjoyed it. But as she drank her coffee she felt an old, sick anticipation clutch at her stomach, and knew that there could be no more putting off the inevitable.

'André . . .'

'Yes?'

The clipped impatience of his tone made her pale slightly, but she persisted. 'We have to talk.'

'Yes.'

'Just like that?' she snapped.

His eyes gleamed with something very like malice. 'Yes, my dear, just like that.'

She turned on him, but he was watching her with such naked amusement that she realised he had wanted her to lose her temper. With an effort that must have been obvious she snatched back control, and turned away to look out over the incredible view.

After a moment, he said calmly, 'Why didn't you want to marry me, Kate?'

So, he wanted to know it all. For a moment she held back, pain and antagonism pushing up beneath her surface control, then, suddenly, she capitulated. Think of it as exposing an inflammation to the cleansing light of the sun, she advised herself with a hard practicality.

She drew a deep ragged breath. 'I couldn't bear to do it. You see, I was in love with you and you were not in love with me.'

There was another grim little silence. She didn't look at him; both had turned their eyes to the great crags of the hills that were Coromandel's spine, deep blue-purple against the sky, forbidding and beautiful.

He said calmly, 'But I was in love with you. Ridiculously, shamefully, passionately in love with you. Why do you think I was so cruel to you? Not because I hated you, although I indulged in a little of that, too. But because I went cold-bloodedly to seduce you into my bed, and found that I had fallen headlong into love.'

To hide her trembling she shoved her hands deeper into the pockets of her coat. 'It was passion,' she said in a colourless voice.

'That, too. I wanted you the moment I saw you, dancing like a houri. That innocent, bold sensuality made a slave of every man in the room. I wanted to carry you off so that you never danced again for any man but me. But passion I could have dealt with; I'd felt it before. It was the realisation some weeks later that I was falling in love with you that shook me. Because I had to avenge poor Olivia. Whatever I did, I'd betray one of you.' She flinched and he smiled, the bitter smile of a man in torment. 'Yes. I loved my stepmother; she had always been kind to me, and after the offhanded attitude of my own mother she was like warm rain on a desert. When Olivia died she had a nervous breakdown, and that fuelled my desire to punish someone. And I loved Olivia, the way a man loves someone too weak to survive alone. She relied on me to look after her.'

'I'm sorry,' Kate said hopelessly.

'So am I. But perhaps that will explain why I behaved so badly. Until then I had always been in control of my emotions. And, of course, I realised very early on that you were too young to love me.'

Her eyes fixed on to the hills as though they were her lifeline to reality. 'Oh, I loved you,' she said in a low voice. 'Too much, André.'

'Did you? I wonder. I'm sure you thought you did.'

Still not looking at him, she said quietly, 'Afterwards I told myself that it hadn't been love. It was the only way I could cope with the pain.'

'That's why I didn't follow you after I'd seen you in his bed. Although it was like being flayed, I knew that I had to let you go. I thought I'd frightened you so much that you had to run to another man. Whatever might have happened if I hadn't been seduced into acting like God, with the right to take vengeance, by then it was too late for it. So I let you go.'

'You let me go because you thought I was sleeping with Brent,' she snapped, her spirit surging back. She turned to scan the forceful lines and angles of his face.

'I wonder if he ever knew how close to being killed he was that night?' He was staring up at the hills, his eyes narrowed so that she couldn't discern his emotions. 'Why did you go to him, Kate?'

Her hands clenched. 'I was afraid,' she said in a small, ashamed voice.

'Why not tell me the truth?' Now he looked at her, his eyes narrow slivers of jade. 'You hated what we did——'

'Oh, don't be an idiot! With you it was all fire and crystals and beautiful perilous seas, a kind of ferocity that stripped me of all the civilised emotions and left me with only the wanting.'

'Was it, Kate?' Incredulously she watched as the hard mask of his features broke into a swift vulnerability. 'Then why did you go to Brent bloody Sheridan?'

'Because you talked of marriage but you hadn't said a word about loving me. Think, André! I'd watched Chris with Olivia, falling deeper and deeper into love, betrayed, laughed at, cuckolded, he the lover, she the one who was loved. Oh, I didn't know whether you would be cruel like her, but the prospect of being like Chris, hopelessly, abjectly in love with a man who only *wanted* me filled me with such horror—all I could think of doing was running. But when you rang—I knew that you could talk me into marrying you, I was weak and all you had to do was look at me and I wanted you! One kiss, and I'd have given you anything you wanted!'

'You didn't have to sleep with Sheridan,' he snarled.

She grabbed him by the upper arms and shook, hard. Immovable, solid as a rock, he looked down at her, his mouth a thin line, his gaze stark and unforgiving in the kindly sun.

'Listen,' she spat, 'for the last time, because I am never going to say this again, *I didn't sleep with him.* I ran, yes, I'll admit to that. I hadn't taken much in the way of clothes when I ran from you, and your telephone call gave me such a fright I forgot to collect any clothes from the flat, so I had almost nothing to wear, and certainly no nightclothes. I got into bed and fell asleep. Brent had a sofa-bed in the sitting-room, and that's where he slept. We did not make love. Not then. *Not ever.*'

His hands snaked out and clasped lightly around her throat. To her astonishment she realised that the lean fingers were trembling. He closed his eyes, then opened them again swiftly, as though trying to catch her out, but she stared up into his hard, beloved face, willing her honesty to shine forth, willing him to take that final step into trust.

He said harshly, 'But he wanted to.'

She nodded, holding the blazing eyes with her own. 'Yes. He asked me to marry him. However, when I refused I think he was relieved. You see, he knew about the baby. I think he would have taken her on, but he wanted to marry a woman he could sleep with, not someone who was morning sick and growing larger every day with another man's child.'

The fingers around her throat tightened, then relaxed. She saw torment in his eyes, and with a muffled sob hugged his taut body to her. 'It's all right,' she whispered. 'André, please don't look like that.'

His arms moved, caught her so tightly against him that she hurt, but she bore the pain stoically, wondering with a hope too long denied whether at last something was going to be right for them.

'So you had to endure all of it—the pain and the shame all by yourself.'

'No.' She lifted her head, speaking urgently. 'No, Libby and Fiona were wonderful, and my parents were too, really, although they thought I'd let them down, and they wanted me to have the baby adopted. They looked after me. They could just have washed their hands of me.'

'Nobody calling themselves a parent could do that. I wish you'd told me. But I suppose I know why you didn't. I don't know that I would have believed you.'

Honesty compelled her to admit, 'Part of it was spite, I'm afraid. Punishing you for——'

'For believing the worst of you?'

'Yes. And for believing Libby when she told you what had happened—you wouldn't believe me. But most of all for not loving me as much as I loved you.'

'But I did. I still do.' His arms eased a little, so that he could push her chin up. For a long moment he stared at her, scanning her face from the cleft chin and soft mouth to the wide, incredulous eyes and the delicate hollows at her temple. 'I believed Libby because I knew, deep down, that you weren't the sort of person who'd lie. You were basically honest. The week we spent together proved it to me. I'd just begun to realise what I'd done to us both, and was trying to work out how the hell I could retrieve the situation, when she arrived, and I was forced to admit I'd been wrong. And I didn't know what to do.' She closed her eyes, and he finished quietly, 'Have you been happy?'

'Yes. Mostly. Happy and—empty.'

In tones that gave nothing away he asked, 'Has there been anyone else?'

She said fiercely, 'You know damned well there hasn't. How about you?'

'No,' he said softly. His eyes narrowed, the heavy lids concealing his thoughts. 'So,' he said casually, 'what do we do about it?'

Her stormy emotions were plain in her face, her chin lifted high as she challenged him. 'We get married!' she snapped.

His face stayed emotionless for at least a second, before the blank mask of control dissolved into his most wicked, most reckless smile. 'How nice to discover that we agree on one thing,' he purred.

His arms were hard and possessive, the kiss hot and persuasive, branding her with a force that should have left her gasping. However, as always, she met and matched his ardour, opening like a flower to the sun of his passion.

When at last he lifted his mouth she said in a stunned voice, 'I can't believe I said that.'

'You did,' he said with immense satisfaction, 'and there's no way you're going to wriggle out of it. I love you. I loved you before I'd ever spoken to you and I loved you through more traumas than Freud ever classified, and I loved you even when I thought you had slept with Brent Sheridan. It was like dying to see you in his bed, as though something had fouled my dreams—and I knew that the something was me and my stupidity.'

She said quietly, 'I'm not exactly proud of myself, either. I knew that you would want to know about your daughter, and I think I probably knew I could convince you that she was yours. But I didn't. I ran away and hugged my anger and my pique to me, and refused to part with them.'

His mouth touched her eyelids, traced the line of her lashes, wonderfully gentle. 'I dreamed of you,' he whispered. 'I still do. I see you dancing, laughing at me, calling to me, but I can never get to you. There are always people blocking the way. Olivia, Libby, Sheridan—and I have to watch as you dance for them. Dear heart, my soul, when I die it's going to be with your name on my lips and your dear face in my eyes...'

A long time afterwards he lifted his head again and stared around the paddock; the blindness lifted from his eyes and he said half beneath his breath, 'No, not here. The grass is too wet, and I refuse to make love to you in the Range Rover. Let's go home, my darling.'

But on the way down the hill he asked, 'How is Fleur going to like having me around? I suppose she'll be jealous.'

Her first instinct was to laugh it off, but she knew that he was right. Fleur would be jealous. 'Yes. She likes you very much but she is used to my constant attention. We'll have to take things slowly in front of her.'

He sent her the sort of look that sent her pulse soaring through the danger level, but agreed, 'Well, I'll do my best, although I'm not a particularly patient man. At least, not where you are concerned.'

She returned the look with interest, smiling a small elemental smile at the dark colour that stained his cheeks.

Fleur insisted on showing her the kunekune pigs. They were delightful, gorgeous little black balls of wiry fur, with round inquisitive eyes and little straight tails. Their mother watched benignly as Fleur petted them again, making the instinctive crooning noises that came when one was confronted by something cute and small and babyish. She was all set to show them the chickens and lambs and calves, but André shook his head, and said cheerfully, 'We'll have a look at them tomorrow.'

She gave him a hopeful look. 'Are we coming back tomorrow?'

'I hope so. I'm coming down for dinner tonight, so why don't you go off with Mummy and make something delicious for it?'

'Chauvinist!' But Kate was laughing.

He grinned and put her into her car, looking at it with disfavour. 'For God's sake drive carefully in this heap of rust. The first thing I'm going to do is give you something that looks as though it will hang together further than the next four pot-holes.'

She lifted her chin but her expression was serious as she drove down the road. His words had made her remember that not only was he the man she loved, he was also extremely rich. What sort of life would they be living? The thought of wasting her time on an idle social round filled her with dismay; there was so much, she realised, that she didn't know about the man she was going to marry.

It niggled away while she prepared dinner, and must have shown in her expression because the first thing he did after he had kissed her was to say, 'It's no use you changing your mind. You're mine now, and I'm never going to let you go.'

'I don't want to go,' she objected. 'Only——'

His mouth crushed her words, fiercely shutting out the world as though he could bind her to him with the sheer force of the physical magic between them. They remained locked together for a timeless time, until a voice impinged, high-pitched and curious.

'What are you kissing each other for?' Fleur demanded, her expression as close to jealousy as it had ever been.

André crouched down. 'Your mother and I are getting married,' he explained gravely.

Fleur looked warily at him, before asking, 'Are you going to be our new daddy?'

'Would you like that?'

She considered, watching him with his own eyes, her head a little on one side. Then she nodded. 'Yes. Will you be living with us?'

'You'll be living with me,' he said, holding out his arms. Fleur hung back, her little face anxious as she looked from her silent mother to the man she had taken for her friend. André smiled, that charming, irresistible smile, and Fleur's face broke into a grin as she hurled herself at him, her arms closing in a fierce bear-hug around his neck.

'Right,' he said, rising to his feet with his daughter held fast in his embrace. He looked from her entranced face to Kate, and lifted his brows at her. 'Let's go and plan a wedding,' he commanded.

'I want to be a bridesmaid,' Fleur said instantly, clearly totally reconciled to the idea.

André chuckled and dropped a kiss on to her cheek. 'Of course you can be a bridesmaid,' he said with a teasing, beguiling smile. Then his eyes travelled to Kate's face, still a little abstracted. 'Don't go changing your mind,' he said quietly but with total determination. 'I wouldn't be feeling exactly kindly if you put me to the trouble of changing it back for you. Although——' as the brilliant smile broke through '—perhaps I might!'

They ate dinner with Fleur, allowed her to stay up later than usual while they made plans for a small quiet wedding in Whitianga, and a week's holiday.

'I know,' Fleur said importantly. 'A honeymoon. I'll stay with Emma.'

André looked at her with a gleaming smile in which there was something a little wondering, as though he was continually startled at his new status as a father. 'Do you stay with Emma often?' he asked lazily.

'Lots.' Her expression lit up. 'Can I tell her tomorrow, Mummy? Can I?'

'May I?' Kate corrected automatically.

Fleur giggled. 'Yes,' she said with great kindness. 'Of course you may if you want to, Mummy.' Her eyes met André's with something of his own wicked amusement.

Kate laughed deep in her throat. 'Come on, sweetheart, it's time for bed.'

It took longer than normal, but at last they got her there, and asleep, and came back into the sitting-room. It wasn't really cold enough for a fire but André had lit one. Without speaking, he bent to put some more wood on. She sank into the sofa, watching as he stood dusting his hands.

He turned, saw her eyes on him. There was a moment of heavy silence, and then he said quietly, 'Don't look at me like that.'

'Why not?'

'Because it strips me of any control.'

'I don't want you to be controlled.'

He smiled mirthlessly. 'I think that's why I'm afraid of you,' he said conversationally as he came to sit down beside her. 'You threaten me in ways I'm only just beginning to realise. The fact that I love you gives you such power over me.'

'I cede the same power to you,' she said beneath her breath.

He sat, head slightly bent, keeping himself away from her. 'Yes,' he said after a moment. 'That's the only thing that makes it bearable, isn't it?'

She nodded. 'It is frightening. But—it's exhilarating, too.'

He looked up, eyes gleaming. 'Isn't it? You know, I find it difficult to believe that I'm really here, home at last. When you told me that Fleur was mine I was so savagely angry, I couldn't work out what my emotions were. So I went away to give myself a few days without your far too distracting presence. And after doing the hardest thinking I have ever done, I had to admit that, mine or not, it didn't matter. I had been given a second chance, and I was going to take it with both hands. But what shocked me was how much I wanted her to be mine. However, I didn't come back, nor am I marrying you because I believe she's mine. It is you, just you. I saw you again and it all came leaping up out of my subconscious, and before I'd said anything to you I knew we were going to end up like this.'

She smiled, her eyes filling with slow tears, and he gave a muttered curse and pulled her into his arms, holding her close against his taut, warm body until she turned her head and kissed the brown length of his throat. After that it was easy for her to confide her own fears about her life with him.

'There'll have to be some socialising,' he said, 'but I think you'll like my friends. Have you any in Auckland?'

'Yes, both Fiona and Libby are there. Fiona is still single, but Lib and Chris are married, now, and very happy.'

'I liked Fiona,' he said, smiling reminiscently.

Chuckling, she traced the firm contour of his mouth with her finger. 'You and every other man.'

'Guilty. You'll enjoy being closer to them, won't you?'

'Very much.' Dreamily she followed her finger with her mouth, touching his lips with the tiniest and softest of kisses. 'I could go back to university.'

'Would you like to do that?'

She didn't have to think. 'Very much.'

'Good. Do what you like. All I want is for you, and Fleur, and any other children we have, to be happy.'

Her heart swelled. She rested her head against his chest, listening to the steady solid thump of his heartbeat, enfolded in his warmth and the security of his love. Unbidden, unseen, tiny responses sprang into life.

'Speaking of Fleur,' he said casually, 'is she likely to be asleep?'

Demurely she answered, 'We can go and see.'

She was asleep, fathoms deep in the sweet slumber of childhood, a smile curling her mouth. Hand in hand they stood watching her, then left her room and went along the passage to the bedroom. As they went in together she bit her lip, glancing around, trying to see it through his eyes. She had changed the sheets and put flowers, mainly freesias, on the dressing-table and bookshelf, and the sweet evocative scent filled the small white and blue room.

'Don't look so nervous,' he said very softly, turning her so that he could see her. 'I'll go home if you want me to.'

'You dare!' she said fiercely, glaring at him, her eyes spitting golden sparks.

He laughed, and swept her into his arms and on to the bed, hugging her, and then the laughter was joined by passion, and all of her fears and the pain, the loneliness, the last lingering resentments, faded into nothing, swamped by love and laughter and a happiness that might sometimes be altered but would never be lessened.

As they travelled into that land where love was all, heart to throbbing heart, mouth to mouth, bodies joined in ecstatic unity, she thought dazedly that she was glad that she had found no place to hide. For in his arms was home.

my VALENTINE 1992

Celebrate the most romantic day of the year with
MY VALENTINE 1992—a sexy new collection of four
romantic stories written by our famous Temptation
authors:

> GINA WILKINS
> KRISTINE ROLOFSON
> JOANN ROSS
> VICKI LEWIS THOMPSON

My Valentine 1992—an exquisite escape into a romantic
and sensuous world.

◆ *Harlequin Books*

VAL-92-R

Take 4 bestselling love stories FREE
Plus get a FREE surprise gift!

Janet Dailey

Americana

A romantic tour of America through fifty favorite Harlequin Presents novels, each one set in a different state, and researched by Janet and her husband, Bill. A journey of a lifetime in one cherished collection.

Don't miss the romantic stories set in these states:

Available wherever Harlequin books are sold.

JD-MAR